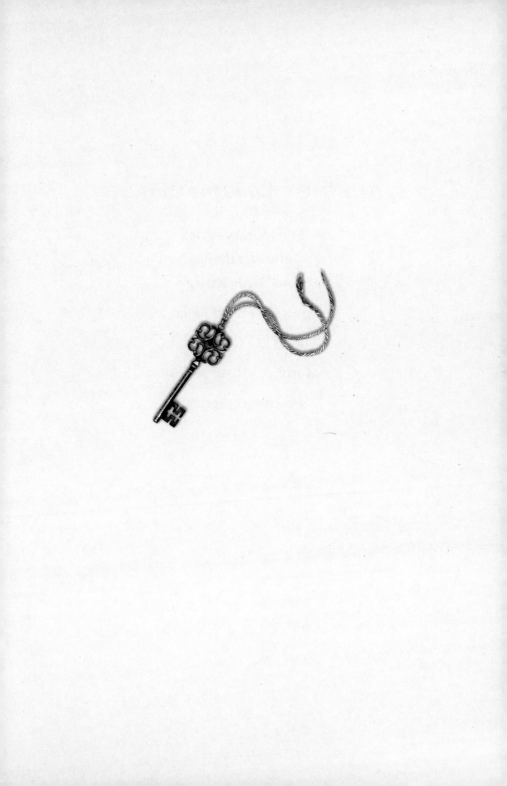

ALSO BY D. J. MACHALE

The Library series
Surrender the Key
Black Moon Rising

Voyagers: Project Alpha

The SYLO Chronicles

Morpheus Road series

Pendragon series

BOOK 3

D. J. MacHale

Random House 🏠 New York

Text copyright © 2018 by D. J. MacHale
Jacket art copyright © 2018 by Vivienne To
Jacket concept copyright © 2018 by Vincent Chong
Key art copyright © 2017 by Bob Bianchini

All rights reserved. Published in the United States by Random House Children's Books, a division of Penguin Random House LLC, New York.

Random House and the colophon are registered trademarks of Penguin Random House LLC. ·

Visit us on the Web! rhcbooks.com

Educators and librarians, for a variety of teaching tools,
visit us at RHTeachersLibrarians.com

Library of Congress Cataloging-in-Publication Data
Name: MacHale, D. J., author.
Title: Oracle of Doom / by D.J. MacHale
Description: New York : Random House, [2018] | Series: The Library. Oracle of Doom ; book 3 | Summary: As Theo's fourteenth birthday approaches, he and Marcus go back in time to meet a fortune teller in hopes of stopping what has been predicted to happen.
Identifiers: LCCN 2017037279 | ISBN 978-1-101-93261-2 (hardcover) |
ISBN 978-1-101-93263-6 (ebook)
Subjects: Supernatural—Fiction. | Libraries—Fiction. | Fortune telling—Fiction. | Amusement parks—Fiction. | Mystery and detective stories.
Classification: LCC PZ7.M177535 Or 2018 | DDC [Fic]—dc23

Printed in the United States of America
10 9 8 7 6 5 4 3 2 1
First Edition

For the Mitchell kids: Allie, Claire, and Teddy,
who aren't really kids anymore
but will always be kids to me

The greatest adventure is what lies ahead.
Today and tomorrow are yet to be said.
The chances, the changes are all yours to make.
The mold of your life is in your hands to break.
—J. R. R. TOLKIEN, *THE HOBBIT*

Eenie meenie, chili beanie.
The spirits are about to speak.
—BULLWINKLE J. MOOSE

FOREWORD

I've written a million stories about middle school kids. (Okay, that's an exaggeration. The truth lies somewhere between a hundred and a million. Closer to a hundred. But, hey, that's still a boatload of stories!) The question is, why? What is it about middle school kids that I find so fascinating?

That's easy. Middle school kids are ready to explode. (Not literally. Though I can think of a few who should probably be detonated.) What I mean is, at that age you're old enough to start getting around on your own. You're no longer joined at the hip to your parents and can actually go out and do things without having an adult watching your every move. That's a big responsibility. It means you could choose to do things your parents might not necessarily approve of, like physically entering books of unfinished supernatural stories and thereby setting yourself up for an untimely and gruesome death. Most parents probably wouldn't go along with that. Mine would have, but that's a whole 'nother story.

When an author is writing about characters who are enjoying this newfound freedom, there are countless options for unique adventures. So why do I write about kids, when anybody can have an adventure?

That's the other half of the equation. Middle school kids are just starting to figure things out. About life, I mean. The real world is opening up and reality is coming on fast. It's not always pretty, but it's definitely exciting. Many kids think they've got it all wired. They're sure they know exactly how life works. And they might, from the perspective of a little kid. Trouble is, they aren't so little anymore. When they hit middle school, they suddenly realize there's a whole new set of challenges to grapple with. In other words, their simple lives get complicated very quickly.

And that's the sweet spot. The place where reality meets fantasy.

Reality is having to face the challenges that come with everyday life.

Fantasy is what you find in a place like the Library.

That's where I live, lying in wait, ready to take un-suspecting kids who are dealing with their normal lives and callously throw them into a roiling cauldron of con-fusion where logical rules don't apply. Does that make me evil? Maybe. A little. But I have to admit, it's kind of fun.

Oracle of Doom is the third book in The Library se-ries. Hopefully, you've read the first two, but if you haven't, don't worry. You'll get up to speed quickly. (Of course, after reading this book, I can't imagine that you wouldn't want to run right out and catch up on the other two. That's okay. I won't hold it against you for being late to the party.)

Many people helped bring these books to you: Diane Landolf, Michelle Nagler, Mallory Loehr, and all the good folks at Random House Books for Young Read-ers; my team of Richard Curtis and Peter Nelson; my blondie girls, who I love for all sorts of reasons, but one is that they accept the fact that my job is all about imag-ining how to put young people through a myriad of tor-turous trials; the many librarians and booksellers who support my books; and, of course, you: someone who enjoys reading about how I put young people through a myriad of torturous trials. Does that make *you* evil? Maybe. A little.

A great big thanks to you all.

That's all from me. Off we go. There's a new book sitting on the shelf of the Library that's gathering dust, waiting for you to discover it. If you recall (or even if you don't, because you haven't read the first two books, you slacker), from the very beginning Theo and Lu have had extra incentive to help Marcus navigate the stories they find in the Library. Of course they want to help their friend and the people trapped in the unfinished stories, but they also fear that they may be going through strange disruptions of their own. One of the unfinished volumes in the Library might very well be about them. They've tried not to stress over it because so much has been happening with the other stories. But they can't ignore the truth any longer.

Unlock the door, crack open the book, and start reading.

This is their story.

Hobey-ho!

—D. J. MacHale

Prologue

Opening day.

Two words that herald the start of something fantastic, whether it's the beginning of baseball season, the grand opening of a new store ...

... or the first day of operation for a spectacular new amusement park.

Saturday, May 1, 1937. The gates opened to Playland Amusement Park, a colossal fun park in Connecticut on the shore of the Long Island Sound. The line of eager customers was already hundreds deep by the time the steel gates were rolled back to reveal the wonderland of brand-spanking-new attractions. The excited guests were greeted by the monstrous Tornado roller coaster; the high-speed Derby Racer; a fun house with a three-story indoor slide; the Laughing in the

1

Dark spook house; the Magic Castle of thrills; Ye Olde Gold Mine tunnel of love; the Whip; a carousel; and, of course, a midway packed with concession stands that offered tasty snacks, as well as game booths that beckoned the daring to step up and test their skills.

The enthusiastic crowds were also treated to a variety of exhibitions meant to dazzle and amaze. A lady high-diver made the hundred-foot plunge from a tiny platform into a shallow pool of water; a troupe of Broadway performers demonstrated energetic dances called the Lindy Hop and the jitterbug; a big-band orchestra played popular swing tunes; and a cast of cavorting clowns kept the littlest visitors laughing (and in some cases, crying in fear).

The most intriguing attraction by far was in an orange-and-white-striped circus tent that stood in a remote area of the park. It had its own special spot beneath a towering oak tree, far from the clang and clatter of the rides. The relative quiet was critical to set the stage for the wonders and magic to be found within. When curious spectators entered the secluded tent, it was like stepping into another world. Another domain. Another dimension.

It was the world of the Oracle Baz.

"Welcome!" a deep, disembodied voice boomed from crackling speakers as visitors filed in for the next show. "Make no sudden moves. Keep young ones close. There's no telling what peculiar perils may be unleashed should the aura of the spirits be disturbed."

The visitors mostly snickered at the ominous warning, but they lowered their voices in reverence just in case, while young kids stuck close to their parents.

Colorful tapestries hung everywhere, accented by a jungle of tropical palms. It made the tent feel as though it were nestled in an exotic oasis instead of an unremarkable suburban town. The stage was a raised platform decorated with artifacts that could have come from Ali Baba's cave or King Tut's tomb. There were brass goblets resting on ornate wooden tables, colorful hand fans, a large gong, and bowls of succulent fruit. A golden birdcage held a beautiful white dove, surrounded by several lethal-looking curved swords that seemed to float in the air.

Sitting prominently at center stage was an ornate throne-like chair with a large letter *B* carved into its back.

Eerie flute music completed the air of mystery for the wide-eyed visitors who filed in and crammed together on long benches, having left the raucous excitement of the park behind to enter this strange inner sanctum.

The lights dimmed. The music died. There was a long moment of silent anticipation and ... *boom!* An explosion of smoke erupted from beneath the throne, making everyone recoil in surprise. The stage was enveloped by a white cloud that quickly blew away to reveal that the seat was no longer empty. Sitting tall on his throne and looking every bit like a regal king was the star:

The Oracle Baz.

His chin was held high as he arrogantly surveyed the assembled gallery. He wore a flowing, deep purple robe with golden trim and a scarlet turban adorned with an exquisite green emerald the size of a golf ball. Most of his fingers sported rings with equally stunning gems. As impressive as his costume was, it was hard not to be drawn to his face. He had a neatly trimmed mustache and goatee, along with penetrating dark eyes that seemed to be gazing directly into the minds of all those who dared to enter his domain.

Most of the spectators let out an awe-inspired gasp at the sight of him.

Baz didn't react, as if it was beneath him to acknowledge their existence. He raised his hand, and the flute music returned. He stood and flicked his other hand, and a long, curved sword appeared from nowhere. He grasped it expertly and swept it back and forth, slicing the air between him and his audience.

The people in the crowd laughed nervously and then applauded.

Baz didn't acknowledge their approval as he moved to the golden birdcage that held the white dove. In his free hand appeared a black cloth, which he deftly draped over the cage. He swung the lethal-looking blade back and forth, raised it high, and, with a sudden violent thrust, drove it into the cage.

Several people yelped in surprise and horror.

Baz let them suffer, but only for a moment. He whipped the cloth away from the cage to reveal that the dove was no longer there. A moment later, the white bird flew from the back of the tent and came to rest on his outstretched palm. The crowd erupted with applause as Baz casually pulled the sword from the cage and returned the bird, unharmed, to its perch.

The sword magically disappeared, only to be replaced by a glass ball the size of an orange. He rolled the orb back and forth from hand to hand, creating the illusion that it was weightless. It was an impressive trick, until the ball actually went weightless. It floated up from his palm and hung in the air like a soap bubble.

The crowd tittered and whispered.

A second glass orb appeared, joining the first in midair. They spun around one another as Baz waved his hands above and below them to prove there were no invisible strings.

Everyone cheered with delight.

The moment they erupted, Baz scowled and dropped his hands to his sides. Instantly, both orbs fell to the floor and shattered, spewing shards of glass across the stage.

The audience fell into stunned silence. Baz stared out over the crowd with a raised eyebrow as if blaming them for having broken the spell.

"The aura of the spirit is not to be taken lightly," Baz scolded in a deep, commanding voice. "Nor is it to be applauded like a cheap parlor trick."

Nobody reacted. Nobody so much as breathed.

"I know why you have come," Baz declared. "And it is not to be amused by trivial feats of magic. You are here to catch a glimpse of the future."

He spun around and returned to sit on his throne. In front of him was a low table with a black cloth draped over it.

"I am but a conduit," he announced. "I do not choose what will be revealed. That will come from you, but only if the spirit aura chooses to display your truth. I do not know if these revelations will bring comfort or warn of great misfortune. If any here today have reservations about what you may see or hear, now would be the time to leave." Nobody did.

With one quick move, Baz yanked away the cloth to reveal a clear crystal the size and shape of a bowling ball. Multiple spotlights hit the orb, giving it a sparkling, otherworldly glow. With a dramatic flourish, Baz waved his hands over the glass sphere and gazed into its depths.

A light appeared from within that reflected in Baz's dark eyes. He focused on it, as if he could actually see something inside the orb. The spectators leaned forward, trying to catch a glimpse of what it might be.

"Landolf," Baz announced. "Diane Landolf. Rise."

A teenage girl near the front of the room squealed with delight and jumped to her feet.

"This is an important moment for you, miss," Baz declared. "On this day you will meet your true love."

The young girl giggled and clapped while her father grabbed her by the sweater and yanked her back down into her seat. He wasn't as thrilled about the news as his daughter was.

The crowd chuckled and buzzed with nervous energy, then quickly fell silent, waiting for the next prophecy.

"Daniel Cook," Baz called out.

A man in the second row tentatively got to his feet. He looked nervous, as if afraid of what might be coming.

"Congratulations," Baz announced. "Your wife, Michelle, is with child."

The woman sitting next to Cook let out a surprised yelp. The man looked down at her, questioning. She gazed up at him with wide eyes and nodded an enthusiastic yes.

"Ye-ow!" Cook exclaimed, and hugged his wife with joy.

The crowd burst out in spontaneous applause. Baz glared at them. Just as quickly, they fell silent.

Baz returned his gaze to the crystal ball and instantly frowned. Whatever he was seeing, it wasn't good.

"I...I...This is quite indistinct," Baz said, finally showing emotion. Whatever he was seeing disturbed him. "I will not lie; I sense the coming of an enormous tragedy. I see a colossal explosion and flames. It will be sudden and violent. Someone here today...someone among us...will be deeply affected by this. Fear not, though. This person will be unharmed. I cannot say the same for many others."

A deep rumbling of concern went through the crowd. Up until then everything had been in fun. Hearing predictions of a violent, deadly accident yet to happen put a definite damper on the show.

Baz threw up his hand for quiet.

"Charlie Simmons!" he called out.

A man no older than twenty was standing at the end of one bench. He wore work clothes, which set him apart from most of the adult men, who wore suits and ties.

"Yeah?" Simmons called out.

Baz stared deep into the crystal and scowled. "You are employed here at the park?" he asked.

"I'm on break," Simmons replied. "It's allowed."

"Go home," Baz snapped. "Do not return to your duties today."

"I said, it's allowed," Simmons said, annoyed. "I can come to the shows."

"I don't care what your superiors have authorized you to

do," Baz snarled. "If you remain here at the park, your life will be in grave danger."

Muffled gasps came from everywhere.

Simmons stood awkwardly, staring at Baz. He finally steeled himself and called out, "I ain't leaving work just because you want to put on a good show. That ain't right. I earned this job."

"And if you want to keep it, you will go home," Baz said with a sneer.

Simmons took a few steps toward Baz, his anger growing.

"What kinda scam you runnin' here?" Simmons shouted. "Those other people you talked about–they friends of yours?"

People looked to Cook and the Landolf girl, who vehemently shook their heads.

"I don't believe it," Simmons said. "You can't monkey with people's lives. Maybe you're the one who's in grave danger."

Simmons took another step toward the stage. Sensing a fight, people sprang up to get a better look. A few men jumped in to hold the angry guy back. Things were about to get ugly.

Baz wasn't shaken. A bright light appeared inside the crystal ball, growing quickly and flashing so brightly that everyone in the tent had to cover their eyes. A few seconds later, they dropped their hands to see that the stage was empty.

Baz was gone.

The surprised emotions were all over the map. People were stunned, they applauded, they shouted in anger, they laughed. Like it or not, the show was over. It might have been a short performance, but it was filled with drama.

Simmons stood near the front of the stage, his fists clenched.

"Hey, fella, you gonna go home?" a guy asked him.

Simmons looked unsure of how to answer.

"Nah," he finally said, and spit on the ground. "If anybody's gotta be worried, it's that phony swami. He better not cross me."

Simmons stormed for the exit as people cleared a path for him.

Once he was gone, the rest of the audience filed out of the tent, abuzz over what they had witnessed. Could Baz actually see the future? Several approached the young Landolf girl and the expectant couple to verify they weren't part of the show. They assured all who asked that they were not plants and had never met Baz before.

Outside the tent, Simmons strode away quickly.

"Charlie!" a woman called as she hurried after him.

Simmons kept moving as the young woman caught up and matched him stride for stride.

"Maybe we should go home," she said nervously.

"It's a joke, Laura," Simmons said curtly. "For show.

Nothing's going to happen, except I might give that Baz character a knuckle sandwich."

"But what if–?"

"I need this job, Laura. We need this job. I ain't leaving."

"Then be careful, okay?"

Simmons stopped and gave her a kiss on the forehead. "I will," he said. "Go have some fun. It's opening day!"

Simmons hurried off, leaving his young wife standing alone and not as confident as her husband that all would be fine.

———————

SIMMONS WORKED ON A ride called Blackbeard's Galleon. It was a massive pirate ship that "sailed" on an artificial waterway that circled the park. The experience was made all the more impressive by sword-fighting pirates who would swing from the masts and do battle on the deck. It had already become the most popular attraction in the park.

Simmons was one of the shore crew. They dressed as pirates, complete with hats emblazoned with a skull and crossbones. Their job was to keep the guests safe and orderly, which was no easy task on opening day, since the ship was filled to capacity on every voyage. The floating dock that was the boarding area was constantly loaded with excited people waiting their turn.

As the giant ship neared the dock, its tall masts could be

seen moving through the trees, looming closer. The "pirates" on board cast heavy lines to the shore crew, who would lash them around metal cleats to stabilize the vessel. It was about as thrilling and dangerous as a Kiddie-Town ride, but the sheer size of the ship was the real draw. The pirate battles were fun too.

After waiting on a very long line to board the ship, the crush of eager voyagers grew impatient. It was a challenge for Charlie and his crew to keep them back. Nobody expected the crowds to be so huge. And unruly.

"Please step back," Charlie urged, trying to keep too many people from pushing onto the floating dock. "Everybody will get on."

It was a hot day in May, and patience was wearing thin. By the time people got to the front of the line, they were more than tired of waiting. Their anticipation only grew as the large galleon finally arrived at the dock. There were squeals of excitement from the youngest kids and a surge from behind as people shoved ahead to get onto the already overloaded dock.

"Don't push, folks," Simmons called out, trying to maintain a welcoming smile. "You'll all get to ride."

The dock listed to one side, causing a small panic.

"Whoa, whoa!" Simmons called out. "I need some folks to step back off the dock."

The float was dangerously overloaded and imbalanced.

Some people jumped back onto the cement landing, but others steadfastly refused to give up their spots.

"Heave ho, matey!" a pirate called from the ship.

That was the signal for the shore crew to be ready to receive the lines and tie up the vessel.

Simmons was torn. The massive ship needed to be secured, but the crowd was getting out of hand. He thought fast and pushed his way through to get to his station on the dock. The pirate on board tossed him the line, and Simmons expertly lashed it around a metal cleat. Done. Within seconds he was back working crowd control.

"We need folks to step off the float," he called out with more urgency.

Nobody got off. More stepped on. The floating dock had been tested for safety long before the park opened, but never with so many people on it. It bucked in the water as people jockeyed to stay on their feet and not go over the side.

"Step off now!" Simmons shouted, his frustration finally showing.

This time people listened. Several stepped back onto the cement jetty, and the float settled down.

Simmons relaxed. Disaster averted. The other shore worker approached him, wiping nervous sweat from his forehead.

"That was close," the guy said. "We need a lot more staff on busy days."

"That's for sure," Simmons said. "Stick it in the suggestion box." With a chuckle, he turned to the ship, ready to pull out the gangplank.

"It's okay, folks," the other worker announced to the crowd. "Blackbeard's Galleon will be back in half an hour for anybody who doesn't get aboard for this voyage."

A disappointed groan went up from the crowd. That wasn't what they wanted to hear.

"Half an hour?" one guy yelled angrily from the rear. "I've already been waiting an hour!"

"It's a big boat!" a mother yelled as she pushed her young children back onto the floating dock. "There's plenty of room!"

"I ain't waiting another minute!" a teenage kid snarled, and leapt onto the dock.

Others followed suit.

"No!" Charlie yelled while throwing his arms out to stop them.

It was no use. Several people jumped onto the dock, making the float list dramatically.

Charlie yelled, "Step off! Now!"

The dock tilted toward shore, putting extra strain on the lines that were securing the ship. They instantly went as tight as guitar strings. It was a strain the ship wasn't designed to take . . .

. . . and a disaster nobody anticipated.

Crack!

A heavy metal cleat was torn from the wooden hull. Like a wild snake, the line whiplashed toward shore, along with the chunk of sharp metal it was attached to.

"Look out!" Simmons shouted, and dove for a young boy who was on the edge of the dock, staring up at the ship in awe.

Simmons pushed the boy out of the way just in time.

The kid was saved.

Simmons wasn't.

The cleat whiplashed through the air at the end of the line and hit him square in the forehead.

The horrified cries from the crowd said it all. They cowered away and finally jumped off the dock. In seconds, the floating platform was cleared.

Only one person remained.

Charlie Simmons. He lay flat, not moving.

The crowd stared in stunned silence. It was eerily quiet except for the joyous sounds of the amusement park that now seemed a world away.

The passengers on the ship lined the railing, staring down at the scene. Some backed away in horror. Others couldn't take their eyes off the disaster. One woman made her way to the railing, looked down to see Charlie, and fainted.

It was his wife, Laura.

ON THE OTHER SIDE of the park, the Oracle Baz's tent was empty. There would be no more shows that day. Baz sat on his throne, staring into the crystal ball.

One of the circus clowns burst into the tent and ran up the aisle toward the stage.

"Hey, did you hear?" the clown called to Baz. "One of the pirate guys got hit with the rigging from the ship. Killed him on the spot."

"Indeed?" Baz said with no emotion. "Mr. Simmons should have heeded my warning."

The clown gave him a curious look. "You, uh, you saw that coming?" he asked.

Baz raised his gaze to focus on the clown. "Perhaps you would like to hear details of your own future?"

The clown's garish face fell. He swallowed hard and backed away. "Uh, no thanks, pal," he said, his voice cracking. "I'll be surprised."

Baz watched the clown scamper away, then turned his attention back to the crystal ball.

"And to think," he said to himself with a bemused smile, "this is but opening day."

CHAPTER

1

I had to see it for myself.

Reading about something is one thing. Experiencing it in person is a whole 'nother ball game. That's why right after school I rode my bike to downtown Stony Brook and hopped on a bus headed west along local streets. I'd taken this same bus a bunch of times with my family and a couple of times with friends. I knew the deal. Ten stops ahead and two towns over was my destination.

Playland.

It was early November. Connecticut snow was still a few weeks away, but it was getting dark early, and the chilly wind that whipped through the barren trees felt like an ominous warning. Halloween was over. The holiday season was coming on fast, and so was another long gray winter.

It had been only a few days since we finished the story we titled *Black Moon Rising*. My friends and I needed a break. We were tired. Simple as that. When we stepped into an unfinished story, time in real life stood still. That was cool, except our bodies didn't stop, and it wasn't like we were sitting around with our feet up playing *The Legend of Zelda*. Oh no. We had just done battle with a centuries-old coven of witches bent on wiping out an entire town and taking over the world.

That took some effort.

After we left *Black Moon Rising* through the interdimensional crossroads of the Library, we wanted nothing more than to rest, recharge our batteries, and spend a little time in the real world before tackling the next story.

Wasn't going to happen.

Another book came our way, and it looked to be the most important one yet. It wasn't about people who lived far away from us, or strangers who existed in the past. No, this story was about my best friends, Lu and Theo, and about a fortune-telling machine that was spitting out predictions that came true.

You know. That.

Both my friends were dealing with strange troubles

known as disruptions. The Library is filled with stories like theirs. Stories that defy logic, that can't be explained using the normal rules of science and nature.

Lu's cousin Jenny Feng was missing. She had left home a few weeks ago, and nobody had heard from her since. It was a total, terrifying mystery. In Theo's case, he had gotten a fortune from that strange machine that told him life as he knew it would end on his fourteenth birthday. Yeah. Seriously. He wouldn't have thought twice about it except both of his brothers had received fortunes from the same machine, and both of those predictions came true.

Everett the librarian had been searching through the stacks in the Library, looking for unfinished books that might contain Lu's and Theo's stories. If he found them, it would mean they were dealing with actual disruptions, and we'd have some information that would help us solve them.

It took some time, but Everett found it.

It. One book. Not two. One.

It held *both* stories.

The book told the tale of an old-time fortune-teller named the Oracle Baz, who supposedly could see into the future. Baz was long dead. He hadn't told a fortune in decades, but the arcade machine with his name on it was keeping up the tradition. Theo and his brothers got fortunes from it, and, as it turned out, so did Lu's cousin Jenny. It was all written in the book. We needed to find out if Jenny's fortune had anything to do with her disappearance, and what kind of trouble Theo might be headed for on his birthday.

We hadn't been dealing with their problems until then because, to be honest, we didn't know what to do. But once Everett found the book, we had information. Now we could act.

And it had to be fast: Theo's birthday was only a few days away.

That's why I found myself on a bus on a cold November afternoon, headed to Playland, the home of that mysterious machine.

I didn't tell Lu and Theo I was going. I wanted to see this magical fortune-telling machine for myself. My friends are awesome—the best—but sometimes I need to think things through on my own. There would be plenty of time for them to get involved. Heck, they were already involved. It was their story.

The bus pulled up to the stop at the end of Playland Parkway, and I was the only passenger who got off. Not a whole lot of people visit Playland in the winter, since it's closed for the season. The bus driver gave me an odd look. I knew he was dying to say, "You know the park is closed, fool. Right?" But he had a schedule to keep, and so he drove off without a word, leaving a cloud of noxious diesel smoke behind.

I'd been to Playland dozens of times. It was a totally familiar place. But seeing it in winter was a whole different experience. The normally leafy trees were barren and gray; the vast parking lot was empty; and there wasn't another person to be seen anywhere. Maybe eeriest of all was the sound. Or lack of sound. Ordinarily, there'd be music and the clatter of rides and screams of excitement from a thousand happy people. But in November it was dead quiet. It didn't help that the sun was on its way down and shadows were growing long. There's a reason why so many horror movies are set in abandoned amusement parks. These places are usually full of life and excitement, so when they're quiet and empty, they just feel . . . dead.

I half expected to see Scooby-Doo and Shaggy run by.

There was a collapsible metal gate pulled across the tall archway that was the entrance to the park. I was relieved to find that it wasn't locked. All I had to do was push it open a few inches to slip through. It was way too easy to get in, which made me think the park probably had all sorts of other security, like cameras and guards and motion detectors. For all I knew, somebody in a high-tech control center had already spotted me, and a team of armed security goons was on the way to toss me out. How would I explain that all I wanted to do was check out the fortune-telling machine?

I had to be stealthy, so I hugged the buildings, staying near pillars and signs and trees and anything else that would block me from view. Moving through the empty park was both creepy and cool. It was like walking through a still frame; nothing was moving. And it was cold. November cold. It gave new meaning to the term *freeze frame* because I was definitely freezing. I wished I had worn something heavier than my usual Stony Brook Middle School green hoodie. I didn't even have gloves and had to pull up my hood to protect my ears. It probably made me look more like a lurker up to no good, but . . . too bad. I was freakin' cold.

There were a couple of arcades in Playland, and I was pretty sure which one was my target. It was a small arcade tucked behind the bumper car building. Nobody went there much. Or ever. It was out of the way, and all the games were retro. I don't mean *Pac-Man* and *Donkey Kong* classics; we're talking dusty vintage games that had been around since Playland first opened. It was more like a museum than an arcade. I think it appealed to grownups because it reminded them of the olden days. You never saw any kids in there; playing those games got boring after about five seconds. I'd been there a grand total of once, and only because I got lost looking for a bathroom. But I remembered it. If there was any place that would have an ancient fortune-telling machine, it would be that dusty arcade.

Being in the park was like having one foot in the present and one in the past. Playland had some seriously great modern rides, like the Jetstar roller coaster and a couple of virtual-reality space adventures. But in addition to all the modern rides, there were still some that had been around since the park first opened. Classics, I guess you'd call them. The Tornado roller coaster was a big old wooden thing that was just as fun as any of the modern metal ones. The Derby Racer was like an out-of-control merry-go-round that spun so fast you had to hang on tight for fear of getting tossed off the horse. There was a tunnel-of-love boat ride called Ye Olde Gold Mine, and the Whip, and of course a Ferris wheel.

Lots of the decorative structures along the midway looked like they'd been around forever too. Arches and wooden sidewalks and food stalls gave the illusion of what the park had been like decades before. There was even an old-fashioned boardwalk lined with games of chance that ran along the shore of the Long Island Sound on the far edge of the park.

What Playland *didn't* have were some of the rides described in the unfinished book that Everett had found. There was no fun house or Magic Castle. There wasn't a pirate galleon that floated on an artificial river. There wasn't even a river. I tried to imagine where the waterway for Blackbeard's Galleon might have been. My guess is it followed the same route that now held a miniature-train ride that circled the park.

I bet they'd ripped out the boat ride because that worker was killed on opening day.

As I stood on the edge of the midway, seeing the park both as it is now and as it had been nearly a hundred years before, I felt a strange tingling sensation that made the hairs on the back of my neck go up. I hadn't heard or seen anything, but the feeling was unmistakable.

I wasn't alone.

Was it a security guard? Or a hidden camera looking down on me from one of the old-fashioned streetlamps? I glanced around quickly and didn't see anybody. But the feeling was too strong to be my imagination.

I was being watched.

I backed toward the closest building, looking for a shadow to sink into, and found myself in front of one of the oldest attractions in the park. The Hall of Mirrors. I hadn't been in there since I was six. It was kind of hokey, to be honest. But in that moment I wanted to be out of sight, and that cheesy attraction seemed like the perfect place. So I jumped over the turnstile and ducked through the entrance.

They should have called it the Hall of Windows—most of the attraction was a maze of clear glass walls that you had to find your way through. There were plenty of twists and corners and dead ends, and if you went too fast, you ended up walking straight into a glass wall and smashing your head. Usually, there were so many fingerprints (and nose prints) on everything that it was easy to find the right way, but on that day the glass was clear and clean. Workers must have squeegeed everything when the park closed for the season.

Maybe I was being paranoid, but I still had the sense that I was being watched. It was more a feeling than anything else. I hadn't heard anything specific, but I felt as though somebody else was in there. In the maze. With me. My heart thumped hard. I hadn't even gotten close to the arcade and I was about to get my butt thrown out of the park. I moved quickly through the corridor of glass with my hands out in front of me to keep from smashing into anything. It wasn't easy. I kept bashing my fingers against the hard surfaces before finding the turns. Whoever had created this ride was evil. How was this supposed to be fun? I was halfway to the center when . . .

. . . a shadow moved by me.

I saw it. No question. It was a person. I only got a glimpse out of the corner of my eye, but the person was real. I couldn't tell where they were or where they were going because there were so many layers of glass all around me. Worse, the only light was what bled in through the front entrance. I was all sorts of disoriented. Was the person in front? To the side? Behind me? It was impossible to tell.

The shadow moved by again, at the edge of my vision. Somebody was definitely there. I spun around, but too late. Whoever it was came and went like an eyeblink. I thought of calling out, but that would have ended my mission for sure, so I kept quiet and continued moving. The tension made it even harder to work my way through the maze because I kept nervously looking over my shoulder, expecting to see somebody standing right behind me.

I finally reached the halfway point. It was a long room that was the true Hall of Mirrors. The corridor-like room was lined with tall, narrow mirrors that distorted your image, making you look really tall or fat or giving you a big head or whatever. Those things are fun for about eight seconds. At that moment they weren't fun at all. I moved through quickly, barely glancing at my reflection as I passed each mirror. I didn't stop. I wasn't in the mood to see myself looking like a munchkin. Or a daddy longlegs. The room was so dark I could barely make out the doorway on the far side.

I was halfway through the hall when I passed the middle mirror and . . .

. . . I thought I saw something strange. It made me stop short. What was it? Had I seen the reflection of another person in the mirror? I glanced over my shoulder, but nobody else was in the room. It must have been my imagination. Or a trick of what little light there was. Or even my own reflection. But I had to know, so I took two tentative steps backward until I was directly in front of the mirror.

My reflection made me look like Shrek . . . wide and grotesque. There was no other reflection besides mine. The mirror faced another on the opposite wall, which made an infinity effect. The reflections bounced back and forth, creating the illusion of hundreds of mirrors trailing off to forever. Normally, I loved that effect.

But this wasn't normal.

Something moved deep within the reflection. It was the silhouette of a person. It wasn't right next to me or behind me but looked to be floating through one of the reflected mirrors deep in the background, which was

27

impossible. It had no features. It was a shadow. But what could be making it? There were no lights. You needed light to make a shadow.

It was impossible, but I saw it. I know I did.

And I didn't want to see it anymore.

I took off running, headed for the exit. The route out was pretty much the same as the way in. It was another maze of glass walls. This time I didn't worry about being quiet or stealthy or bashing into anything. I wanted to be gone. I kept slamming into the glass walls, my shoulders taking most of the hits, but I didn't stop. I saw another shadow float by beside me, but I didn't know if it was real or just my imagination in fourth gear. I didn't care either. The maze grew lighter as I got nearer to the exit, so I was able to see the glass walls more clearly and stopped slamming into them.

When I rounded the last turn before the exit, my fear shifted from what was behind me to what I might find outside. Would I run straight into a cop? Or a security guard? At that moment I kind of hoped for either. I didn't want to be alone with a lurking shadow anymore.

I skirted the final glass wall and blasted out to the midway to see . . . nothing. Nobody was there. No cops. No security. No shadows. I was all alone. Somehow that felt even creepier than if I had been followed by a cop.

What had I been seeing? Or feeling? Did it all happen in my head?

I wanted to run the heck out of there and go home, but I forced myself to take a deep breath and calm down. Nothing had happened. I had probably seen my own shadow reflected in the glass. That had to be it.

And I couldn't leave. The whole purpose of my trip would be lost. I had to keep going. So I sucked it up and headed across the midway to the bumper car ride.

Once there, I jumped the rail that got to the walkway that surrounded the track. The track itself was enclosed by a chest-high wall. The colorful cars were lined up along the wall inside, nose to tail, parked for the winter. I jogged around the oval, hoping that my memory was good and that the antique arcade was still behind the building. When you came out after riding the bumper cars, you'd take a right to head back to the midway. But if you went left, you'd find a narrow sidewalk that looped behind the building. I followed that sidewalk, rounded the corner, and saw the doorway I'd hoped for.

Heritage Arcade.

The old-fashioned, swooping script letters were painted over the door, just as I remembered. I grabbed the handle, and after a moment of fear that the door might be locked, I pulled it open.

29

I can't say I remembered much about the arcade. I'd been there only once before and hadn't been impressed, but in general it was as I'd expected. There were ancient nickelodeons and baseball batting games where, for a nickel, a metal ball would shoot out of a miniature pitching mound and you had to hit a button that would swing a tiny bat at it. I saw a couple of old-school pinball machines and another gizmo that let you control a creepy clown marionette. That one was good for a few nightmares. I suppose some historian would find the whole thing fascinating.

I didn't. There was only one machine I cared about.

I walked past several of the dusty games, rounded a few corners, doubled back, and was beginning to think I had struck out when I made one last turn . . . and came face to face with the Oracle Baz.

Or at least a dummy replica of him. It was the biggest machine in the place. The life-sized mannequin was sealed inside a glass booth. You could only see him from the waist up because he sat at a table that held a big crystal ball. His hands rested on either side of the globe as he stared into its depths, supposedly gazing into the future.

Hanging on the wall behind the machine were a couple of giant vintage posters that advertised *The Oracle Baz,* probably from back when Baz had actually put on shows at the park. For real. Yellowed paintings showed him standing dramatically with his feet apart and his hands held out like he was conjuring spirits. Phrases were spelled out in bold letters across the artwork: *ASTOUNDING!, GLIMPSE INTO THE FUTURE!, FEATS OF MAGIC!, ENTER IF YOU DARE!,* and various other slogans and come-ons with exclamation points, designed to entice people into his show.

That show had closed a long time ago. Now there was only a glass box and a dummy.

Sitting on the table next to the crystal ball was a wooden box filled with fortune cards. I figured the way it worked was you put in your quarter and the dummy Baz would pick out one of the cards that told your future and would drop it into a slot. It was all pretty lame and harmless . . .

. . . unless of course your fortune said you were going to die on your next birthday. That would kill the joy of a fun day at the park, and no amount of cotton candy would make it right.

To say the gizmo was creepy was an understatement. The dummy was dressed exactly as he was described in the book from the Library. He wore a purple robe with gold trim. On his head was a fiery-red turban with a giant green emerald stuck right in front. I wondered how accurate his face was. He definitely looked mannequin-like, with a waxy, dark complexion.

His glass eyes were deep and black, his mustache and beard were neatly trimmed, and each of his fingers had a fancy ring.

What really got me, though, were his intense, un-wavering eyes. They were glass, I got it, but they seemed so real. I couldn't stop staring at them. I knew he was a wax dummy, but I swear I expected him to blink.

It was a profoundly eerie moment . . .

. . . until I heard the crunch of a footstep on the concrete behind me. It might have been faint, but the arcade was so quiet it sounded as loud as a gunshot.

Somebody was standing right behind me.

"Enjoying your visit to the park?" a man's deep voice asked.

I wasn't alone after all.

CHAPTER
2

I spun around quickly and came face to face with a man wearing a navy-blue security guard uniform. He was an older guy with silver hair and bright gray eyes to match. I guess I should have been scared, seeing as I had just been busted, but the smile on the guy's face made me think he was cool. He didn't have a gun either. That was a plus.

"Come to have your fortune told?" he asked.

"Uhhh . . . yeah," I muttered. "Something like that."

I thought about bolting for the exit, but it wasn't like I was doing anything wrong—except for the whole trespassing thing, that is. Running would just make me look guilty, and there were probably other security guards hanging around who weren't as easygoing as this guy, so I didn't move.

The old dude chuckled. "Usually, when folks sneak into the park, they head for the spook house. Or hunt for food. Lately, they've been taking selfies in front of signs to prove they were here. But coming to this old arcade, well, that's a first."

He didn't seem like he was going to have me arrested or anything, so I relaxed a little.

"I'm not messing with anything, Eugene," I said, because that was the name on his name tag. "Can I call you Eugene? I'm Marcus."

"Sure, Marcus," he replied with a shrug. "But you ain't gonna be here long enough for us to be pals."

"I know. I just wanted to get a look at this thing."

I jabbed my thumb at the fortune-telling machine and immediately wished I hadn't, because Eugene's friendly smile dropped. I had said the exact wrong thing.

"Really?" Eugene said suspiciously. "Now, why is that?"

I looked at the dummy of Baz as if the wise oracle could help me out, but all he did was stare into his crystal ball with his glassy, lifeless eyes. Thanks for nothing, chief.

"I'll tell you, but you won't believe it," I said.

"Could it be that you had a fortune come true?" Eugene asked.

I gasped. I really did.

"Okay, maybe you *will* believe it," I said, barely above a whisper.

Eugene stepped up to the machine and stared through the glass at the Baz dummy.

"I've been working here awhile," he said. "It's easy work and I love Playland. Always did. Spent a lot of time here when I was a kid. Seen lots of changes; heard lots of stories. Did you know they wanted to shut down this arcade and turn it into a Dippin' Dots?"

"That fakey ice cream?" I asked.

He chuckled. "Thankfully, enough people who love the park squashed the plan. That's one of the beauties of Playland. Its history. You see it in the buildings and attractions that have been around since the beginning. As much as it keeps pace with modern times, it also shows respect for the past. Nowhere more than here in this arcade. Hardly anybody comes by anymore, but when they do, they walk away with a true appreciation for the spirit of the park and all that it was, not just what it is today."

The guy was getting lost in his memories. It was sweet and all, but I needed him to focus on the present.

"So you heard stories about this machine?" I asked.

"The Oracle Baz," he said with reverence while looking up at the posters. "He was a real fellow—did you know that?"

"Yeah. I heard he really could predict the future."

"So they say. Unfortunately, he didn't predict his own."

"Why? Did something bad happen to him?" I asked.

"Sure did. He lived in an apartment over a dark walkthrough attraction called the Magic Castle. About two weeks after the park opened, there was a fire. The attraction burned to the ground. Baz was trapped in his apartment. He never had a chance."

Whoa. I hadn't gotten that far in the book.

"He died?" I asked, surprised. "Here? Same as that pirate ship guy?"

"How does somebody your age know about that tragedy?" Eugene asked, with a puzzled frown.

"I read a lot" was my vague but entirely accurate answer. No way I wanted to tell him about the Library. "How do *you* know so much?" I asked.

"I guess you could call me the unofficial historian of Playland," he replied. "I told you, I love this place. I pretty much know every square inch of the park."

"How did the fire start?" I asked.

"They never found out for certain," he said with a shrug.

"So that means somebody might have set it."

Eugene shot me a look of surprise, as if he hadn't thought of that. But thinking like that was my job. If stories ended up in the Library, there was always a good reason. A simple accident wouldn't qualify. It had to be something strange that happened—something that somebody did, or didn't do, or should have done. A disruption. Disruptions didn't happen by accident, and a mysterious fire that killed somebody sure seemed like a disruption.

Eugene shrugged and said, "Maybe. It's a mystery that'll never be solved."

Bingo. Disruption.

"Don't be so sure about that," I said.

He gave me a curious look. "What makes you say that?"

"No reason," I replied innocently. Again, I wasn't going to tell him about the Library.

I think I was gaining his trust. Hopefully, that meant he wouldn't call the cops on me.

"You're right about Baz," he said. "From what I understand, the fella had a genuine gift. Look here," he said, pointing to the machine. "That's the actual costume he wore onstage. And that crystal ball—it's the very same one he used to make his predictions. They saved all his props and built this machine."

I gazed into the dummy's lifeless eyes that were intently focused on the crystal ball. I half expected him to wink.

"That's all his real stuff?" I said in awe. "Isn't that a little—I don't know—creepy?"

"I suppose," Eugene said with a sigh. "He was only here a short time, but he helped put Playland on the map. He was already famous, so it was a big deal that the park got him to come. It was a publicity stunt, I guess, but it worked. People flocked from all over to see his show. Him dying was horrible, but it made the park famous. Or maybe . . . notorious. Either way, you couldn't keep people away. Building this machine was a way to honor his memory and keep the people coming. If not for him, Playland might never have caught on the way it did, and we could be standing in a shopping mall right now."

"Or a Dippin' Dots."

Eugene gazed around at the antique games as if they were beloved grandchildren. He really did have a thing for this park. Odd, but whatever.

"So what about the fortunes?" I asked again, prodding.

"Mostly it's rumor and legend, with a little bit of embellishment tacked on, but I've heard more than once that fortunes spit out by this machine ended up coming true. I can't say for certain how real it is, but I do know this old machine is somewhat . . . particular."

"How so?"

"It doesn't always work. Oftentimes people put in their quarters and nothing happens. Baz just sits there staring into his crystal. The maintenance folks have taken it apart more than once, trying to figure out what makes it work. Or *not* work. It's a fairly simple mechanism. But most times it just . . . fails. The story goes that the only time Baz will tell a fortune is when he has a fortune to tell. Doesn't matter if you put in a quarter or a dozen quarters. If Baz doesn't see anything in your future worth mentioning, he won't."

"You talk about him like he's real," I said.

Eugene had been staring at the dummy of Baz. He tore his gaze away to look at me.

"Do I?" he said. "Silly. It's just a machine. Then again, the stories seem real enough. Folks say that whatever magic Baz had somehow found its way into this machine."

"Do you believe that?" I asked.

Eugene laughed at the idea. "Not really. But it is kind of fun to imagine, don't you think?"

"Not if the machine spits out a fortune that tells your best friend he's going to die."

39

Eugene's look turned dark. "Is that what happened?" he asked, suddenly concerned.

"Yeah. I wanted to see this thing for myself. Not sure why. It's not like I can ask Baz to step out of that box and tell me how to protect my friend."

"You sure about that?" he asked, staring at the ground thoughtfully.

"Huh?"

"Got a quarter? Maybe Baz can see into *your* future."

I looked back into the creepy eyes of the dummy. Did this thing really work? Did those dead eyes really see things? I reached into my pocket to grab a quarter but quickly pulled my hand back out, empty. What if Baz told me something about my future that I didn't want to know? Besides, this was about Theo. And Lu's cousin. Not me. At least that's what I told myself. Was that being selfish? Or just plain chicken?

"I'll pass," I said.

Eugene shrugged and said, "Up to you."

"So those stories you heard," I said. "Were there times when the fortune *didn't* come true?"

Eugene scratched at his chin, thinking back. "Can't say I'm an authority," he said. "But from all I've heard, if Baz saw it, there wasn't a whole lot you could do to change it. Or so the legend goes."

That was the last thing I wanted to hear, and I guess Eugene saw it in my face.

"I'm sorry, son," he said. "Don't worry about it. They're just stories."

That didn't make me feel any better. I knew the power of stories.

"I hope you're right," I said.

"Let's go. I'll walk you out of here," Eugene said. "Come on back another time, when the park is open."

He turned and headed for the exit. I followed right behind him.

"You know you totally freaked me out before," I said.

"What d'ya mean?"

"In the Hall of Mirrors. I thought you were a ghost or something."

Eugene stopped short and I nearly ran into him.

"You went into the Hall of Mirrors?" he asked. "Today?"

"Well . . . yeah! I knew somebody was following me, and I didn't want to get thrown out before I saw the Baz machine."

"Son, the first time I laid eyes on you was when you were headed into the arcade. I didn't go into the Hall of Mirrors."

"So it was another security guard," I said.

"I'm the only one on duty. You and I are alone in the park."

"But . . . I saw somebody," I said, stunned.

"Who knows?" Eugene said with a mischievous wink. "Like I said, lots of history in this park. Maybe some of it's come around to pay a visit."

He turned away and continued for the exit.

My head was swimming. No way I was imagining things. Someone had followed me into the Hall of Mirrors. I thought this was going to be a story about fate and fortune. Could it be I'd found myself in another ghost story?

I turned around to get one last look at the fortune-telling machine . . . and my knees went weak. Maybe it was the angle or a trick of the light, but it sure looked real. I stood looking down the corridor formed by the old-fashioned arcade machines to the glass box that held the Oracle Baz.

He was no longer staring into his crystal ball.

He was looking square at me.

CHAPTER

3

"The Oracle Baz died in a fire two weeks after opening day," I said. "Can you believe that? Two weeks, two deaths. Unbelievable."

"Yikes," Lu said with dismay. "That's like the most unamusing amusement park ever."

I closed the black leather-bound book with the story of the Oracle Baz and laid it down on the circulation desk in front of Everett. We had all come to meet with him in the Library. Lu, Theo, and me.

It was time to deal with their disruptions.

"Maybe the Magic Castle fire that killed him was the big disaster Baz had predicted during his show," Lu said.

"I don't believe so, lass," Everett said. "Read what

happened just a few days after he made that prediction." He opened the book and slid it across the desk toward Lu and Theo.

Theo didn't look at it. He hadn't said a word since we got there. I couldn't blame him. We were trying to figure out if he was going to die on his fourteenth birthday. That would tend to put anybody on edge, especially if your birthday was only a few days away.

Lu eagerly grabbed the book. While she read silently, I kept my eyes on Theo.

The guy was brilliant. His mind worked like a computer. Talking to him was like talking to Siri on an iPhone, except he actually came up with useful information and you didn't have to repeat yourself twelve times before he understood the question. I was surprised that his normally logical mind was twisted up over a fortune that had come from a machine. Then again, I wasn't the one who'd been warned about my imminent death. I probably shouldn't judge.

"No way," Lu exclaimed, looking up from the book. "Is this true?"

"The books don't lie," Everett said. "Besides, the event wasn't exactly a well-kept secret."

"What does it say?" I asked.

"Playland opened on May the first, 1937," she replied, referring to the book. "On May the sixth, the *Hindenburg* zeppelin exploded and burned in New Jersey. Thirty-five people died. One of the guys working the lines on the ground had been to Playland on opening day. He survived, just like Baz predicted." She lowered the book and looked at us. "That's just . . . strange."

I glanced at Theo.

He looked sick.

"Okay, so this Baz guy got a couple of things right," I said. "But he couldn't have been all that good, or he would have seen his own future and saved himself. And even if he really had some kind of psychic power, I don't buy that it jumped out of his head and into a machine."

"You're being thick, boy-o," Everett said, sounding frustrated with me. When Everett was worked up, his Irish accent got stronger and his bald head turned red. I'd have been afraid he was going to have a heart attack, except he was already a ghost. "You read the book. That machine has been spitting out fortunes that have come true for decades. We can't ignore that."

"But it's crazy," I argued. "It's a machine."

"Aye," Everett said. "It is crazy. Completely crazy. Same as all the other unfinished stories on these shelves. If everything that happened in this world was always neat and logical, there'd be no need for the Library. I should think you'd know that by now."

Theo kept his eyes on the floor and didn't even tug at

his ear, which was something he did when he was working through a problem.

"What do you think, T?" I asked.

Theo took a deep, thoughtful breath and said, "I can't speak for Lu's cousin because I don't know what her fortune said, but I think I'm in real trouble."

"Seriously?" I shouted quickly. "You believe this fortune-telling stuff? That's, like, so not you."

"On the contrary," Theo said. "It's exactly like me."

"I don't get that," Lu said.

"I'm not sure I get it myself," he said. "But there appears to be quite a bit of evidence that says it's real. And if it is, what if the predictions can't be changed? What if it's all predestined?"

"That's just stupid," Lu said dismissively. "The future hasn't happened yet. Anything can be changed."

"But what if a prediction takes into account that somebody's going to find out and try to change it? The very things you do differently could lead directly to causing the event that you're trying to avoid."

"Well, that's disturbing," I said.

"So what are you saying?" Lu asked in frustration. "You want to hide under your bed and not do anything to try and protect yourself?"

"No, I'm saying it might not matter what I do," Theo said, downhearted.

"Well, I'm not gonna sit around and let fate take control of my life," Lu shot back. "Or my cousin's. Or yours, whether you like it or not."

Theo started tugging on his ear. The guy was genuinely freaked.

We all turned to Everett, hoping he would offer some words of wisdom.

"If Baz died under mysterious circumstances, chances are this is his story," he said thoughtfully while tapping the book. "But there's more to it than that. The disruption that took his life seems to have affected people ever since then, right up until now, with Theo and Lu's cousin Jenny. The book describes hundreds of fortunes and predictions that came true. We can't ignore that."

"I don't care about all the others," Lu said. "I want to keep Theo safe and find my cousin."

She grabbed the book and flipped to a page that Everett had marked. "All it says about Jenny is that she got a fortune from the Baz machine in September. It doesn't say what it was or if it came true."

Everett took the book back from Lu and flipped through a few pages.

"She's one of a very long list of people who received fortunes," he said. "Theo's on that list too. Most of them don't have any more details than that. But there are enough that do to make me believe we have to take it seriously."

"So the spirits who write these books don't always write about everything they see?" I asked.

"They do, but they aren't all-knowing," Everett replied. "If they were, there would be a lot fewer unfinished books on these shelves. We're the ones who have to fill in the gaps, and there's only one way to do that."

He snapped the book shut and dropped it onto the circulation desk. It hit hard, like an exclamation point at the end of a sentence.

"We finish the story," he said.

Lu and I stared at the book as if it might magically flip open and spill its secrets.

Theo looked at the floor. I think he was trying not to cry. Or puke.

"Too bad we can't talk to Baz," Lu said. "He could look into his crystal ball and tell us what's really going to happen."

I was suddenly feeling guilty about not putting a quarter into the Baz machine. Weenie.

"Who says you can't?" Everett said, as if it was the most obvious statement in the world. He reached out and slid the book toward us.

Lu and I stared at it for a few seconds, not sure of what he meant.

It dawned on me first.

"We have to go into the story," I said.

"Aye," Everett said with a sly smile.

"But Baz died early on. The story goes right up to the present. It's not like we can jump back into the beginning of the book, when he was still alive."

"And why not?" Everett asked.

Lu and I exchanged confused looks.

Everett reached under the counter and pulled out a scarlet bookmark, complete with a golden tassel.

"Place this mark anywhere in the book," he explained. "When you leave the Library, that's the part of the story you'll enter."

"You mean we can go back in time?" Lu asked, incredulous.

"No," Everett said. "You can go to any time in the story. The tales in these books exist in their own world. Their own reality. It's not the same as actually going back in time."

"That's not how it worked with *Black Moon Rising*," I said. "That was all happening in the real world."

"Because that story was unfolding in the present," Everett explained. "Baz's story happened decades ago, like most of the stories on these shelves. The disruptions that happened in the spirits' actual lifetimes keep them from resting in peace. That's why their stories are here. I

49

don't believe Baz will rest in peace until the truth about his death is known. That's where we come in."

"You think it was Baz's spirit I saw in the Hall of Mirrors?" I asked.

"Can't say for sure," Everett replied. "And we won't know until the story is complete."

"But what about the present?" Theo asked in a soft voice. "My birthday hasn't happened yet."

"Find that truth from the past," Everett replied. "It might help us learn about what's happening in the present."

The three of us stared at the closed book as if it would offer some advice to help us know how to do that. For the record, it didn't.

"There's a whole lot about the Library we still don't understand, isn't there?" I said.

Everett shrugged. I took it as a yes.

I had hoped that my trip to Playland earlier that day would have given me some answers, but all it did was raise more questions. I wanted to solve this mystery and help my friends without jumping into another insane story, but I was kidding myself.

I knew what we had to do.

"Lu," I said, "go to your aunt's house. Maybe you can find the fortune card Jenny got from the machine. If we

know exactly what her fortune was, it might help us figure out what happened to her."

"All right," Lu said. "What about you guys?"

I looked at Theo. He still looked sick.

"We may not be able to change the past," I said. "But
we have to be able to control things that haven't happened yet."

"That's what I said!" Lu exclaimed.

Theo gave me a hopeful look, but his worried eyes
told me he wasn't as sure about it as I was.

"T and I are going to Playland," I said. "In 1937."

"We are?" Theo said weakly.

"Now you're talking, lad!" Everett exclaimed with
glee.

He quickly took a fountain pen from beneath the
counter, handed it to me, and opened the black book. I
think he wanted to act fast, before I changed my mind.
Glued inside the cover was a blank lined card.

"First things first," Everett said. "You need to check
out the book."

I knew the routine. To enter the story, I had to sign
out the book. It's what I had done when we finished *Black
Moon Rising*. But that story was happening in the present. This new story mostly took place almost a hundred
years ago. It was strange enough to know that entering

the world of these books would transport us to another place; the idea that it could also transport us to another time, another dimension, added a whole 'nother layer of weirdness to the festivities.

A really cool layer of weirdness.

I took the pen without hesitation and signed my name.

Everett blew on the ink to dry it, then flipped through a few pages.

"I'll mark the book to a time before the fire. It's hard to be exact, but it should give you enough time to find Baz and talk to him before . . ." His words trailed off.

"Before he dies," Theo said, completing the thought.

"Finding out how the fire started will help complete this story," I said. "But I want to get to Baz and have him take a look into the future."

"You mean *my* future," Theo said.

"And my cousin's," Lu added.

Everett placed the red bookmark between the pages and slapped the book shut.

"Good luck, lads," he said.

I stood and rounded the counter, headed for the door on the far side of the Library that would open into the story. Theo was right behind me, followed by Everett and Lu.

I stopped in front of the ancient wooden door and

stared at it. On the other side was another story, another mystery, another time.

"Ready?" I said to Theo.

He straightened his bow tie and stood tall. "I suppose so," he said with false confidence.

"Give my regards to the olden days," Lu said.

I grabbed the doorknob and hesitated. We were about to leave this reality and step into another. There was no way to know what we would find on the other side, and to be honest, I couldn't wait.

I heard music coming from beyond the door. It was faint, but unmistakable.

"Carousel music," Theo said.

I couldn't help smiling. This was really going to happen.

"It's Playland," I said. "Let's go play."

I yanked open the door, and the two of us stepped through the portal into another dimension.

CHAPTER
4

We stepped through the door into a workshop that was cluttered with tools and machine parts. The strong smell of grease and oil burned my nose hairs while the cheerfully wheezy sound of calliope music filled the room.

"Convenient how the Library sends us to out-of-the-way places," I said. "This must be where the maintenance guys work."

"Looks like it," Theo replied. "I don't know what we'd do if we stepped out into a crowd."

"Hey, who are you?" someone yelled.

Oops.

We spun to see a little kid sitting in the corner behind a workbench, loaded down with carnival snacks.

He had cotton candy, a box of popcorn, a couple of hot dogs, and a bag of peanuts. I wasn't sure if I should be jealous or disgusted.

"How'd you get in here?" the kid asked accusingly. "Only park workers are allowed."

I couldn't tell whether the kid was angry, or scared, or worried that he'd been busted for loading up on junk food.

"Yeah, well, what about you, chief?" I asked. "It's not like you work here. What are you? Seven years old?"

"I'm nine," the kid shot back, insulted. "My parents run a snack stand, so, yeah, I work here."

This kid might have been little, but he didn't back down.

"How do you know we don't work here?" I said, figuring it was better to stay on the offense with this tough guy.

"Doubt it," the kid said. "Unless you're a couple of clowns."

"Clowns?" Theo asked, surprised. "Why would you say that?"

I knew the answer. Theo had on a bright blue shirt with a bow tie and suspenders. It was his usual prep look. I wore jeans, but with a bright green hoodie. This was definitely not standard 1937 wear. The little kid had on a pair of baggy dark woolen pants, a grease-stained white shirt, and a cloth cap with a small brim that made him look like one of those kids you see in movies, selling newspapers on street corners.

In 1937, we were the freaks. I hadn't even thought about how we'd stand out like, well, a couple of clowns.

"You're absolutely right we don't work here," Theo said. "Not yet, anyway. We thought we'd try out to be clowns. That's why we chose this attire. You know, to look like them."

Good old Theo. Always thinking. Even while dimension-hopping.

The kid laughed and took a big bite out of his hot dog. "Yeah, well, sorry. You don't look nothing like 'em," he said with a full mouth. "Those clowns are tough. If they think you're making fun of 'em, they'll kick you right outta here. They don't like it when people don't show 'em respect."

"You mean some people actually show them respect?" I asked.

"Absolutely!" Theo jumped in, stopping me from saying anything else stupid. "We love clowns."

"No, you don't," the kid said. "Nobody loves clowns."

The kid was young, but he was smart. I liked him. He reminded me of . . . me.

"Exactly," I said quickly. "But still, we're gonna try, so we'll get moving."

I started for the only other door in the workshop, figuring it was the way out.

"Take some clothes from that box," the kid said. "The mechanics pinch stuff from the lost and found and take it home to their families. They won't miss nothing."

Theo and I exchanged shrugs and went for the box. We dug through and found a couple of dark sweaters and caps like the one the kid was wearing. We each took a sweater and put it on over our clothes.

"Thanks, chief," I said. "What's your name?"

"Derby," he said while jamming pink cotton candy into his mouth.

"I'm Marcus. This is Theo."

"Don't see too many coloreds here at Playland," Derby said.

"What!" Theo exclaimed, stunned.

"Hey, don't get all twitchy," Derby said. "Don't make no difference to me. Just being observant."

Theo gave me a look that was somewhere between anger and confusion.

"Remember where we are," I said to Theo. "Or *when* we are. It's something people say in 1937."

Theo nodded. He understood but wasn't any happier about it.

We each put on a cap and looked one another over.

"Not bad," I said. "We'll fit right in."

"Want me to take you to the clown tent?" Derby asked.

"Yeah," I replied. "But first we want to see the Oracle Baz."

Derby let out a quick laugh.

"You and everybody else," he said. "Half the people come to Playland just to see him. They're hoping he'll say they're gonna strike it rich or marry a millionaire. They don't like it too much when he tells them they're headed for trouble. And he does tell 'em. Baz doesn't hold nothing back."

"Can you introduce us?" Theo asked.

Derby looked us both up and down. "What's in it for me?" he asked.

Theo and I gave each other questioning looks but came up empty.

"We don't have anything to give," Theo said. "Except for the sincere gratitude of two fellows who are in desperate need of assistance."

Derby glared at Theo through squinted eyes, as if trying to figure out what planet he had just dropped in from, and not just because he was "colored."

"You talk funny," he said.

"Yeah, he does," I added with a laugh. "Makes me crazy."

Derby jammed the rest of his hot dog into his mouth, swallowing it nearly whole.

Theo grimaced as if the sight made him want to gag.

"I like you two," Derby said. "I'll take you to Baz."

"Excellent!" I exclaimed.

As Derby crumpled up the wrappers from his food, Theo reached up for the pull chain that controlled the overhead light.

"Whoa! Leave it!" Derby yelled.

His sudden loud reaction made Theo and me freeze up.

"I was just turning off the light," Theo said tentatively.

Derby hurried for the door. "I don't like the dark is all," he said, calm again. "Wait'll I'm outside."

"Whatever you say," Theo replied.

When Derby opened the door and walked out, we were hit with the full-throttle sound of calliope music from the carousel.

"That was strange," Theo said.

"Leave the light on," I said. "Don't want to freak the kid out."

Theo let go of the pull chain, and the two of us hurried after Derby.

When we left the small workshop and entered the

vast round room that held the carousel, things turned strangely familiar. I felt as if I had just been there because, well, I'd just been there. The carousel was the exact same one I'd ridden dozens of times. It gave me hope that moving around this Playland in 1937 wasn't going to be a totally alien experience.

Wrong.

We stepped out of the carousel building into a totally alien experience.

It was Playland, but it wasn't. I recognized some of the classic rides that were still around in our time, but that's where any similarity ended. The weirdest thing to see was the people. The men wore suits and ties, like they were going to work in an office or something. Many wore hats too. The kind you'd see in old-time gangster movies. All the women wore dresses. Most had on high heels. Even the little girls wore dresses. It was odd to see how they got all fancy just to go to an amusement park. At least the boys wore pants and buttoned shirts. None had on hats or ties.

And Derby was right—there weren't many black people. Actually, I didn't see any at all. There were no Hispanics or Asians either. Weird.

The park itself looked different, but not in a strange way. I guess some amusement parks are just time-less. We walked past familiar booths with games, and concessions selling snacks. The prices were incredible, though. Six cents for a cola and ten cents for an ice-cream cone. I could get used to that. Maybe there really was such a thing as "the good old days."

"It's hot," Theo said. "So incongruous."

I wasn't sure what he meant at first, mostly because it took a while for me to figure out what *incongruous* meant, but it finally dawned on me that it was November. The bookmark had sent us to the part of the story right after the park opened, in May. So we had traveled across time, space, and a couple of seasons.

As we moved through the crowded midway, we passed many rides I recognized. The Tornado roller coaster and the Derby Racers were the exact same, but some of the other rides were long gone by our time.

"Check it out," I said, pointing to the biggest building on the midway. It was made to look like an imposing medieval castle. The words *Magic Castle* stood out boldly above the front doors in foot-high letters. "Scene of the crime," I said. "Or it will be, anyway."

"We've really gone back in time," Theo said, awestruck.

"No," I said. "We've gone into the time of the book."

We stood there, taking in the spectacle, trying to get our heads around the fact that we were actually seeing things the way they had been in 1937.

Theo and I made eye contact, and we both smiled. We were thinking the same thing.

"This is freakin' awesome," I said.

"Hey, you two want to shake a leg?" Derby yelled.

That snapped us back into the moment. We weren't there to sight-see, so we jogged to catch up to the kid.

"Gotta warn you," Derby said. "Baz might not want to talk to you. He's not very . . . I don't know the right word—"

"Accommodating?" Theo asked.

"Friendly," Derby replied. "Not many people like the guy. You might say he's got a couple enemies."

"We don't want to be pals," I said. "We just need a small favor."

"You're dreaming!" Derby said with a laugh.

"Why don't people like him?" Theo asked.

"Beats me," Derby said. "I never hear anybody say anything nice about him. He likes me okay, though. I do chores for him, like cleaning up his stage and bringing food to his apartment. He lives over the Magic Castle. Did you know that?"

"We did," Theo said.

I wanted to add, *Not for long.* But that wouldn't have been cool.

The kid led us off the midway to the far end of the park, headed toward the Long Island Sound. It was much quieter there, since we were away from the crowds and the noisy rides.

"That's where he does his show," Derby said, pointing to a big orange-and-white-striped circus tent sitting under a huge oak tree. "You came at a good time. He doesn't go on for an hour. He likes to be alone before a show. Says it helps him clear his mind so he can consort with the spirits or something dumb like that."

The silence was suddenly broken by a horrified scream that came from inside the tent.

The three of us froze.

"Guess he's not alone after all," I said.

"Is that normal?" Theo asked.

"The screamin'?" Derby said nervously. "Uh . . . no."

"Help!" came another terrified scream.

I took off running for the tent, afraid that one of Baz's enemies might be getting to him before the Magic Castle fire did.

It was looking as though we were too late.

CHAPTER
5

I made it to the entrance of the tent just as a woman came running out, looking frantic. She was wearing a fluffy white bathrobe, and when it flapped open, I could see that she had on a fancy one-piece bathing suit covered with sparkly buttons, like it was a costume of some kind.

She spotted me and grabbed me by the shoulders.

"Stop him!" she screamed at me. "He'll kill him!"

She let me go and ran off, hopefully to get help.

"That's the high-dive lady," Derby said, stunned. "Daring Donna."

Without thinking, I blew past Derby and ran straight into the tent.

The place was empty except for two men standing

on the stage. One I recognized as Baz. He looked exactly
as he did in the posters except he wore a regular white
shirt and dark pants instead of his purple robe and red
turban. The other guy had on denim coveralls. He held
one of Baz's swords with both hands, pointing the blade
directly at Baz's throat. Baz looked pretty calm, considering a sword was waving in his face. Though he did
back off as the guy stalked toward him.

"You are making a grave mistake, my friend," Baz
said calmly.

"I ain't your friend, and this ain't no mistake," the
guy snarled.

"If I were you," Baz said coolly, "I'd worry more
about avoiding runaway trucks than concerning yourself with who the young lady wishes to spend her free
time with."

This only made the denim guy angrier.

"Runaway trucks? You can't flimflam me, and you
ain't never gonna see my girl again."

"Perhaps you should ask her how she feels about
that," Baz said with a smirk.

That was the wrong thing to say. I thought the other
guy's head was going to explode. He reared back with
the sword and let out a guttural yell, ready to strike.

"Hey!" I screamed.

The guy with the sword froze.

Baz didn't even look my way. He was totally focused on the sword, ready to defend himself.

Theo and Derby ran in behind me.

"What's goin' on?" Derby yelled.

The guy with the sword hesitated, not sure of what to do. He looked at us, then at Baz, who gave him an innocent shrug. The guy stumbled back a few steps and dropped the sword to the stage, as if realizing how close he had come to murdering somebody. He then stood straight and pointed a threatening finger at Baz.

"Stay away from my Donna, hear me?" he said through clenched teeth.

"I'll take that under advisement," Baz said. "And do be careful."

The guy jumped off the stage and ran past us for the exit.

Baz watched him run off and spotted us. I expected him to say, *Thank you for saving my life, young lads!* Or something like that.

He didn't.

"The next performance isn't for another hour," he announced snottily.

Derby hadn't been kidding. This guy wasn't exactly friendly. And he had enemies. If we hadn't come in, Baz might have been skewered.

He picked up the sword from the stage floor.

I nodded to Derby to talk to the guy. Or the oracle. Or the fortune-teller. Or whatever the heck he was.

"Hey, Baz," Derby called out. "These fellas wanted to talk to you."

Baz didn't even look our way. He sat on his throne, took out a white handkerchief, and began cleaning the sword, as if to wipe away any annoying fingerprints the guy may have left behind.

"Of course they do," Baz said, bored.

I walked slowly toward the stage. "You okay, Mr. Baz?" I asked. "That guy wasn't kidding around."

"Poor fool," Baz said. "Apparently, he feels as though I've been spending too much private time with the graceful young high-diving lass."

"Are you?" I asked.

Baz gazed at the shiny blade. I couldn't tell if he was admiring the sword or his own reflection.

"Indeed," he said. "Far too much time, I'm afraid. I've grown bored with the Daring Donna."

I looked at Theo. He raised his eyebrows in surprise.

Baz was more than just unfriendly; he was a total jerk. No wonder he had enemies.

"So, uh, Mr. Baz," I said, "could you do us a favor and—"

"Baz!" the guy barked. "No *mister*. I don't ascribe to such pedestrian convention."

"Oh, okay, whatever, Baz. I don't know how the whole fortune-telling thing works, but we were hoping you might take a look into that crystal ball of yours and—"

"Why would I do that?" he asked.

"Well, uh, that's a long story, but we have a couple of problems coming up and—"

"Go away!" he snapped.

"But—"

"I am not a servant for people who are too insecure to weather the natural trials that come with life."

"Uh," I muttered, "I don't really know what that means, but my friend already had his fortune told, and it wasn't very clear, so—"

"Clear?" Baz said. "Life isn't supposed to be clear. It's messy. It's surprising. It's unpredictable!"

"Except that you predict things," Theo said.

Baz glared at Theo. He didn't like being challenged.

"Could you just tell us one thing?" I asked. "Can the future you see be changed?"

"The future is what it is," Baz said. He punctuated the comment by grabbing the sword's handle and stabbing it into the stage at his feet.

"Well, we did kind of just save your life," I said. "So I thought maybe you'd make an exception and take a peek into—"

"Stop!" Baz shouted angrily.

He stood up quickly, as if he'd had enough of us and was building to an anger explosion. The guy was pretty tall, and being up on that stage made him seem like a giant.

"Maybe this wasn't such a good idea," Theo whispered.

"I will not stoop to your level," Baz said through clenched teeth. He stalked toward the edge of the stage and leapt to the dirt floor.

I don't scare easily, by bullies or anybody else, but this guy was seriously intense. He continued walking toward us like a cat stalking its prey. I had to back off.

"I get it," I said, trying not to let my voice crack with tension. "But this is pretty important—"

"You continue to hound me," Baz said. "Apparently, my warnings have not sunk into that minuscule brain of yours."

I bumped into Theo, pushing him backward. Theo bumped into Derby, and we all backed away while Baz kept walking slowly toward us.

"Jeez, we just got here," I said. "It's not like we've been bugging you."

"Perhaps this will convince you," Baz said.

From out of nowhere, a golden dagger appeared in his hand.

"Whoa!" I exclaimed. "Let's not get crazy here."

"My gift is not for sale," Baz exclaimed, his voice rising higher. "Nor am I!"

Baz reared back with the dagger, ready to throw it.

"What're you doing, Baz?" Derby yelled.

Baz whipped the dagger our way.

I turned and tackled Theo and Derby, knocking all three of us to the ground as the dagger spun through the air over our heads.

"Are you nuts?" somebody yelled out.

I looked up from where we were sprawled on the ground to where the voice had come from.

A man stood next to one of the wide wooden poles that held up the tent. He looked pretty slick in a suit and tie, but his eyes were wide with shock.

The dagger was embedded in the pole, right next to his head.

"Get out," Baz yelled to him venomously.

The oracle hadn't thrown the knife at us. It was meant for the guy in the suit. Baz had either missed him or meant it only as a warning.

The guy pulled out a handkerchief, took off his hat, and nervously wiped his forehead.

"You're making a big mistake, Baz," the guy yelled back. "You want to be stuck playing two-bit carnivals and sideshows the rest of your life? Your choice."

"Indeed it is," Baz replied.

"Then you're a fool. Good luck to you, loser. You're gonna need it."

The guy was ticked. I didn't blame him. I'd feel the same way if somebody chucked a knife at me. Because somebody just did. The guy spun and hurried for the exit, all the while glancing back over his shoulder in case Baz decided to wing another dagger at him.

"Who is that?" Theo whispered to Derby.

"Mr. Hensley. The park manager."

"And another Baz-hater," I added.

I pushed off the other two and jumped to my feet. "Look, chief," I called to Baz. "All we want is—"

The stage was empty. Baz was gone.

"Let's go after him," I said, and started for the stage, but Theo jumped up and held me back.

"I don't think that will get us anywhere, Marcus," Theo said. "Not if he's throwing knives at people who ask for his help."

I couldn't argue with that.

"What's Baz got against that Hensley guy?" I asked Derby.

"From what I hear, Hensley wants to be partners with him," Derby said. "He brought Baz to Playland because he was already kind of famous. But Baz wants nothing to do with Hensley. Says he's a solo act."

71

"Who'd want to be partners with such a creep?" Theo asked.

"I don't know," Derby said. "Maybe somebody who wants to see the future."

"We're spinning our wheels here," I said, and stormed for the exit.

When I stepped out of the tent, the first thing I saw was a woman standing about twenty yards away, leaning on a tree, staring at me. Or maybe she was staring at the tent. Either way, it was totally eerie because she looked horrible. She hugged herself like it was cold outside, though it was steaming hot. Her eyes were red and set in dark sockets, probably because she'd been crying. Her hair was a stringy mess, like she hadn't combed it in a week. This was definitely not somebody who came to the amusement park for an afternoon of thrills and popcorn. She leaned against the tree for support, looking so fragile a stiff breeze might knock her over.

I couldn't move. The sight of this strange, haunted woman was, well, strange and haunting. For a second I thought she might be a ghost. Why not? It's not like I hadn't seen any before. And she sure as heck looked spooky enough.

Theo and Derby joined me and both stopped to stare.

"Well, that certainly is unsettling," Theo said under his breath.

"You see her, right?" I asked.

"Of course I do," Theo replied, like it was the dumbest question ever asked.

"Poor lady," Derby said.

"You know her?" I asked.

"It's Mrs. Simmons," Derby said. "Her husband was killed on opening day."

"The pirate boat guy?" I asked.

"Yeah," Derby replied. "Baz predicted something would happen to him. She's been coming to the park every day since. She just kind of wanders around like she's dreaming. Nobody bothers her. They feel so bad for her. I think she blames Baz for what happened."

Mrs. Simmons backed away from the tree and walked off just like Derby had said, as if she was floating through a dream. Or she really was a ghost. Which she wasn't. I think.

"And there we have it," I said.

"What?" Theo asked.

"Another enemy of the Oracle Baz. It's getting to be a long list."

"You guys want to know where the clowns are?" Derby asked.

"No, I think we should go home," I said. "Maybe another time, okay?"

"Sure," Derby said. "Just don't ask me to go with you

to see Baz again. It's getting dangerous to be around him. See ya!"

Derby jogged off, headed back toward the midway.

"It's getting dangerous, all right," Theo said. "Especially for Baz. Maybe one of those people he's having problems with will set fire to the Magic Castle."

"If that's true, and we find out who it is, it might finish the story," I said.

"Baz's story," Theo said. "Not mine. Or Lu's cousin's."

"Let's get outta here," I said, and started for the carousel.

We'd only gone a short way when we passed the park manager, Hensley, headed back toward Baz's tent. Whatever he wanted from Baz, he wasn't going to give up easily. Fool.

A little farther on we saw the guy in the coveralls arguing with his girlfriend in front of a concession stand. It was the high-dive lady. Daring Donna. Or was she Baz's girlfriend? She was crying as the guy stood over her, screaming. Can't say that I blame him. I wouldn't want my girlfriend hanging out with that sleaze.

"Look out!" somebody screamed.

A truck came careening onto the midway, out of control. People shouted in fear and scattered to get away. The denim guy was directly in its path. He turned to face the truck but didn't move, as if he was so surprised at the sight that his brain locked. Donna grabbed him and pulled him out of the way a split second before the truck flew past. It barely missed him, sped on, and finally smashed into a tree.

Nobody was behind the wheel.

A park worker came running up, yelling, "Sorry! Sorry! It got away from me!"

Nobody was hurt, but it had been close.

"Baz predicted that!" Theo exclaimed. "He warned the guy about runaway trucks. He really can predict the future."

I was quickly becoming a believer.

We walked on toward the carousel, passing poor Mrs. Simmons, who sat alone on a bench, clutching something that looked like a pirate hat. She was crying.

The mystery of the Oracle Baz was only getting deeper. We were no closer to figuring out what was going to happen to Theo on his birthday, or where Lu's cousin was, for that matter. But after what I'd seen, I didn't need any more convincing that Baz really did have a direct link into the future.

We had to figure out how it worked. And fast.

CHAPTER
6

ANNABELLA LU WAS ON a mission.

Her cousin Jenny Feng had been missing for several weeks, with no clue as to what might have happened. At twenty-two, Jenny was known to disappear for a few days at a time. She was a free spirit who loved music and followed several bands to their concerts all over the country. She had friends everywhere and often crashed at their houses. There was nothing wrong with what she did, but she usually neglected to tell anybody she would be gone. After her college graduation, she continued to live with her parents in Stony Brook, and they worried about her as if she were still a young child.

"Hi, Aunt Tina," Lu said when her aunt opened the front door.

"Annabella!" Aunt Tina exclaimed. "What a surprise!"

Lu unlaced her roller derby skates and left them on the doorstep. She knew that Aunt Tina liked things to be neat and clean. Rolling around her house on skates would be frowned upon.

"I'm guessing you haven't heard from Jenny," Lu said as the two of them hugged.

Aunt Tina's smile fell, and the worry lines grew more pronounced around her eyes.

"I want to be positive," she said. "It's not like this hasn't happened before. But not for this long without any word."

"What do the police say?" Lu asked.

Aunt Tina shrugged dismissively. "They have no idea. They tried to locate her using her cell phone, but there's no signal. I just don't know what else to do."

Tears welled up in Aunt Tina's eyes, so Lu gave her a reassuring hug.

"Would it be okay if I checked out her room?" Lu asked. "Maybe there's some clue that was missed."

"Please do," Aunt Tina said.

Lu wasn't looking for just any clue. She had a very

specific target ... the fortune card from the Oracle Baz machine.

Lu ran up the stairs to the second floor, taking two steps at a time. Though Jenny was older than Lu by eight years, the two cousins had always been close friends. Jenny was like the cool older sister that Lu never had. She had introduced Lu to all kinds of music and movies and even played roller derby with her for a while. It wasn't until Jenny left for college that the two had drifted apart.

Jenny's room was very familiar to Lu. She had been there countless times. So when she opened the door, she couldn't help but laugh.

"Whoa," she said to herself.

The room was spotless and tidy ... the exact opposite of the way Jenny kept it. Aunt Tina had been busy. Not a single piece of clothing was on the floor, the bed was made, and the bathroom counter was free of makeup.

Lu went straight for the vanity, which had a triple mirror and a padded seat. It had several small drawers, perfect for collecting all sorts of items both valuable and not. Lu had been through the drawers many times. Jenny had no problem with that. She said she had nothing to hide.

Lu went drawer by drawer, yanking them open and digging through years of accumulated junk. She found makeup and brushes, hair clips and a curling iron, vitamins, and notepads. In other words, absolutely nothing out of the ordinary. They could easily have been her own drawers at home.

She turned her attention to several wooden jewelry boxes that rested on top of the vanity. One held just that: jewelry. Jenny had loads of earrings, pendant necklaces, and silver rings. A second box held a stack of instant photos. Lu did a quick scan and saw that they were mostly selfies and casual shots of Jenny's friends and family. There was even one of Lu and Jenny together, making pouty kissy faces. It made Lu laugh and feel sad at the same time.

The third box had more promise.

It held a collection of cards that advertised band performances and parties, along with ticket stubs from concerts that dated back a few years. Lu slowed down and looked at each of them, noting the dates in case one might offer a clue to where Jenny was headed when she dropped off the face of the earth.

When Lu was nearly at the bottom of the pile, she scored.

"Yes!" she exclaimed.

The card, made of heavy paper, was roughly the size of a credit card. It was ivory-colored, with deep brown lettering that gave it the feel of an antique that had been printed a century before. On one side was a drawing of a crystal ball with fanciful writing above it: *The Oracle Baz*.

On the other side was the fortune.

SEIZE THE MOMENT. YOU MAY NOT GET ANOTHER OPPORTUNITY. FOLLOW YOUR HEART.

"Any luck?" Aunt Tina asked. She stood at Jenny's door, looking pained.

Lu quickly palmed the fortune card so her aunt wouldn't see it. It would have been tricky to explain why she thought it was important.

"Not really," Lu said. "I thought maybe some of these tickets might give me a clue, but they didn't. Sorry."

"I'm so worried," Aunt Tina said.

Lu went to her aunt and gave her another hug.

"Me too," Lu said. "But Jenny is going to be okay. I really believe that."

"How can you be so sure?"

"I just have a good feeling," Lu said. "We're going to figure this out."

Lu slipped the fortune card into her back pocket and headed for home.

Mission accomplished.

———————————

"Jenny's fortune isn't scary at all," Lu said, holding out the card she had nicked from her cousin's jewelry box.

"You mean not scary like mine," Theo added, depressed.

"Well . . . uh . . . no," Lu said awkwardly.

The three of us were in Theo's room at his house. It was after dinnertime. Theo had stayed home sick from school, though he was about as sick as I was, and I wasn't. I think he was getting ready to hunker down and barricade himself inside.

His birthday was only two days away.

I took Jenny's fortune card from Lu. " 'Seize the moment,' " I read. " 'You may not get another opportunity. Follow your heart.' "

"That's not a warning," Lu said. "It's advice. It's nothing like . . ." Her voice trailed off.

"Go ahead say it," Theo snapped. "It's not like Theo's."

"Let me see yours," I said to Theo.

Theo handed me his fortune card. It looked exactly the same as Jenny's except that it was worn and dirty. He'd been holding on to it for weeks, rubbing it between his fingers with nervous energy.

" 'Life as you know it will end on your fourteenth birthday,' " I read. " 'Humility.' "

"Humility?" Lu said. "What does that mean?"

"I guess it means I'm going to die and I should be humble about it," Theo snapped. "Swell."

"You're not going to die!" Lu shot back. "We won't let you."

"How?" Theo asked impatiently. "That guy can see the future. I saw it happen. And if his spirit is somehow working through that fortune-telling machine, I'm done for."

"Then we'll change the future," Lu argued.

Theo jumped up and paced, tugging his ear, thinking. Theo was a genius. It took him seconds to work through problems that left mere mortals in the dust. Like me.

"I've been giving this a lot of thought," he said,

turning professorial. "Did you know there are physicists who believe time travel into the future is possible?"

"Uh . . . no," I said. "Except in sci-fi movies."

"But it's true. Even Einstein speculated about the possibility. It has to do with accelerating matter to such a rate that it can break through the ripples of time."

"You mean like with a flux capacitor in a DeLorean?" Lu asked with a chuckle.

"No, like with an atomic explosion," Theo said, deadly serious. "The theory is that if matter were propelled faster than the speed of light, it would speed up time and send that matter into the future."

"Yeah, so?" I asked. "You want to travel through time?"

"No, but it might explain how Baz can see into the future. If he can somehow accelerate light, it might give him a glimpse into what's going to happen."

Lu and I gave each other sidelong glances.

"That's your theory?" I said skeptically. "You think he's got atomic fusion going on inside that crystal ball of his?"

"I have no idea!" Theo shouted, exasperated. "But there *is* scientific theory that says travel into the future is possible. If that's what Baz can actually do, it means he's seeing things that are going to happen. Not that *might* happen—that *will* happen."

"He doesn't see an entire future," I said. "He just sees certain dramatic things."

"Exactly!" Theo exclaimed. "But dramatic things don't just happen. There has to be a series of events leading up to them. It's like fast-forwarding a movie. You can always jump ahead to the big climax, but you'd be missing everything that built up to that moment."

"What's your point, Einstein?" Lu asked impatiently.

"When Baz sees into the future, he's skipping over all the events that led up to a dramatic moment," he explained. "But none of those events actually happened yet, so nobody knows what they are. That means there's no way to know what has to be done differently in order to change the dramatic event."

"So you're saying there's nothing we can do to stop you from being killed the day after tomorrow?" I said.

Theo started to answer, but the words didn't come out. That was because my words were still hanging in the air like deadly, stinking vapor.

"I think that's exactly what I'm saying," Theo finally said, barely above a whisper.

"Bull!" Lu shouted. "That would mean our entire lives are already planned out, and no matter what we do we can't change it. So then why go to school? Or listen to our parents? Or brush our freakin' teeth? It wouldn't matter what we did, because everything's already been decided."

85

"I know it's how you roll, Theo," I said. "But I don't think you can explain any of this through science, any more than we can explain the Library."

"Then why else would Baz see events, if they aren't predestined?" Theo asked.

"I don't know!" Lu said with frustration. "It's magic. Who cares? Whatever the reason, I can't believe we don't have control over our own lives. It would mean this story is about something way bigger and more important than . . . than—"

"Than my death?" Theo said.

"I didn't mean it that way," Lu said sheepishly.

She looked ready to jump out of her skin. She sat in a chair, her leg pumping with nervous energy. She needed to be on the roller derby rink to get out her aggression.

"This isn't an experiment, Theodore," Lu scolded. "You can't input this data into your computer of a brain and calculate it like a mathematical equation. It's beyond science. It's a . . . a . . ."

"A disruption," I said.

"Yes!" Lu yelled. "A disruption. Our job is to figure out how to end disruptions, right? If we can't save you, then the whole human race might as well give up because it means we're all just along for the ride with no say in anything that happens to us."

Theo and Lu looked at each other, both hoping for a better answer. A solution. A solid plan.

Neither had one.

"I don't know if the future is set or not," I said. "But I know how we can find out."

"How?" Theo exclaimed quickly, as if grasping at a lifeline.

"Come with me," I said.

I reached up to the collar of my shirt, grabbed the leather cord that was around my neck, and pulled out the Paradox key . . . the key that had been handed down to me by my biological father, who had also been an agent of the Library.

"Everett doesn't know either," Lu said.

"And I'm not going back into that story," Theo added.

"Yes, you are," I replied. "We're all going back. It may be the only way to save you. You have anything for Lu to put on?"

"What's wrong with what I'm wearing?" Lu asked, indignant.

She had on a short plaid skirt, black tights, and a blue denim shirt.

"Nothing," I said. "Unless you want people staring at you like you dropped in from Mars."

"I have some old pants that don't fit anymore," Theo said, digging through drawers.

He found a pair of khaki pants and a white shirt that looked kind of generic. Lu took them reluctantly and went into the bathroom that was off of his bedroom to put them on.

"And wipe off the red lipstick!" I called in to her.

"I look like a little boy," she said with disgust as she walked out wearing the costume.

"Yeah, you do," I said. "Perfect."

Lu didn't look happy at all. Too bad.

I stepped up to Theo's bedroom door and felt the key grow warm in my hand. As strange as this is to say, I didn't think twice about what was happening. I had gotten used to it. I held the key out toward the doorknob, starting the chain of events that would open the door into the Library.

A small dark shadow appeared on the wooden surface of the door, beneath the doorknob. The wood itself transformed, as if turning liquid. In seconds, an ornate round brass plate appeared. The Paradox key fit perfectly into the keyhole. I twisted it and heard the familiar click of the bolt retracting. I took out the key, turned the doorknob, and pulled the door open to reveal . . .

. . . the Library. The rows of dark shelves filled with thousands of books were becoming a familiar and welcome sight. How weird is that? I made sure the door was closed tight behind us and strode quickly for the circulation desk while draping the key cord around my neck.

"I was afraid you'd given up!" Everett called to us from somewhere deep within the old-fashioned library.

We walked quickly past the aisles of polished wooden shelves that were packed tightly with leather-bound volumes until we came upon the spirit-librarian, who sat reading the black book that held the story of the Oracle Baz.

"I see you've made progress, lass," he said to Lu, peering over his wire-rimmed spectacles at us. "You found Jenny's fortune."

The spirits who observed the disruptions and documented the stories contained in the books were always up to date. Everett already knew exactly what had been going on.

"Oh, *now* Jenny's story is in the book?" Lu said. "About time."

"I believe that's because you're now on the case," Everett replied. "What do you suppose the fortune means?"

"No idea," Lu said. "At least it didn't say she's going to die." As soon as those words were out of her mouth, she winced. "Sorry," she said to Theo.

Theo scowled at her.

"What do you think, Everett?" I asked. "Is the future already written? Or can it be changed?"

Everett closed the book, took off his glasses, and rubbed his eyes.

"I understand Theo's point," he said. "How is it possible to control an event in the future if you have no way of knowing what will lead up to it? But I also believe we are in charge of our own destinies. Free will and all that."

"I told you he wouldn't know," Lu said, scoffing.

It was Everett's turn to scowl at her. Lu ignored him.

"Well, I don't think our lives are planned out," I said. "And I know how to prove it."

I dug under the circulation counter for the 1937 sweaters that Theo and I had dumped there after we left the story. I grabbed the hat I had worn and jammed it on Lu's head.

"They don't have many black people running around that park in 1937, and they definitely don't have any Asians."

"So everybody looks like you?" Lu asked snidely.

"Not really. My hair is way too long."

My hair wasn't long at all. It only came over my ears, but in 1937 all the boys had tight buzz cuts.

"We have to blend in," I said.

"So how do we prove the future can be changed?" Theo asked while putting on his own cap.

I slipped on my sweater and headed for the door that would lead into the story. The others followed close behind.

"Because we know what's going to happen," I said. "Baz is going to be killed when the Magic Castle ride burns down."

"So?" Lu said.

"So we're going to save his life. If we can stop him from being killed, it'll mean we can do the same thing for Theo."

"It doesn't work like that, boy-o," Everett said. "I told you: ya can't be changing things that already happened."

"Maybe not in real life, but we can make changes in the story," I said. "I know we can. We stopped Baz from being attacked by some jealous boyfriend with a sword. If we hadn't been there, a fight would have broken out for sure. We changed the story."

"Is that true, Everett?" Theo asked. "Is that how it works?"

"Aye," he said. "When you're in a story, you're in a different reality. You could save Baz in the story, but like I told you, that won't change actual history, only the version you're visiting. Nothing you do in the story will affect Theo's actual future."

"But it'll prove it *can* be changed," Lu said. "That's brilliant."

"I thought so," I said smugly. "Everett, put the bookmark in a place just before the fire."

Everett flipped through the pages, reading quickly.

"I can't be certain," he said. "The books don't recount every second of every day. But near as I can tell, this will put you in the park on the night of the fire. When exactly it will happen, I can't say."

We reached the door where the faint sounds of calliope music could be heard coming from the other side. I opened it, and the rush of sound from the story hit us like a wave rolling out of the past.

"I smell popcorn," Lu said in awe. "This is so incredibly awesome."

"Okay, then," I said. "Let's go change the future."

CHAPTER
8

Nighttime at an amusement park is a whole different kind of experience than during the day.

Every building was decorated with white lights lining the roofs, making the midway sparkle like a fairyland. The rides were covered with thousands of multicolored twinkle lights that helped create the illusion of magical fun. Strangely, it didn't look much different from the park in the present day. The place was crowded too. Everybody seemed to be having a blast on this late-spring evening. Music mixed with the mechanical sounds of rides, the smell of fried food, and the happy screams of excitement. Some things never change, I guess.

Then again, we were trying to make sure some things *did* change.

Lu pulled her cap down low, trying to become invisible. "I don't know if this is cool or terrifying," she said.

"Cool," I replied. "The terror comes later."

"There it is," Theo announced, pointing.

The Magic Castle ride was the most impressive building on the midway. The soaring turrets of this make-believe castle towered over everything but the Tornado roller coaster.

"What kind of ride is that?" Lu asked.

"I think it's one of those spook-house things where you walk along in the dark and things pop out at you," I replied.

"Baz's apartment must be in one of those turrets," Theo said. "If the place caught fire, there'd be no way out."

We moved through the crowd to get a closer look at the doomed ride. A drawbridge stretched from the midway, over a wide moat of water, and into the arched entrance. There was no line. People kind of walked in whenever they wanted. That was one huge difference from modern amusement parks where you had to wait in long lines for everything. I guess there were a lot fewer people back then.

I walked to the edge of the moat and scanned back and forth. About a hundred yards to our right, on the far side of the park, I could see the masts of the pirate ship known as Blackbeard's Galleon. They rose up above the buildings along the midway, looming like dark, ominous silhouettes. It was the infamous ride where Charlie Simmons met his fate on opening day.

"I suppose that ship has made its last voyage," Theo said.

"So much trouble going on," I added. "Makes you wonder if this park is cursed."

"Don't say that!" Theo scolded. "We've got enough problems."

"Speaking of trouble . . . ," Lu said, pointing.

A group of young boys formed a circle on the grass near the Magic Castle entrance. One kid in the middle was getting shoved around.

"Is that our friend Derby?" Theo asked.

The little guy was being ganged up on by the others. My blood started to boil. Bullies do that to me. I ran across the drawbridge and right up to the gang.

"Hey!" I shouted.

The bully boys froze like I was a cop, but not before one of them gave Derby a final shove that sent him tumbling down onto the grass.

"You guys are real tough, ganging up like that," I said. "How about if I jump in on Derby's side?"

There was a lot of mumbling and foot shuffling as they all backed off in different directions.

"Didn't think so," I added.

One kid got in a last shot at Derby. "Sissy," he said under his breath.

"C'mon, tough guy," I snapped at him. "Let's go."

I took a threatening step toward him, and the kid took off.

Theo helped Derby to his feet. "Are you okay?" Theo asked.

Derby yanked his arm away, embarrassed and angry.

"What's going on?" I asked.

"They think I'm a sissy because I won't go through the Magic Castle alone," he grumbled. "They all did it, but . . ."

He didn't have to finish the sentence.

"But you've got a thing about the dark," I said.

Derby shrugged.

"One on one, I'd knock their blocks off!" he said defiantly.

"I know you would," I said. "Do me a favor? If you're gonna suck it up and go through, wait till tomorrow, okay?"

"Why?" Derby asked.

I glanced at Lu and Theo. They looked away, not knowing what to say.

"Because you don't want to let those little thugs know they got to you," I said.

"Sure, pal," Derby said. "Whatever you say."

He started walking away, but as an afterthought he said, "Hey, you gonna be a clown?"

"Clown?" Lu said, surprised. "You hate clowns."

"Still trying to figure that one out," I said while pushing the others to leave. "See you around, chief. Remember what I said. Don't go in there tonight."

We walked back over the moat and away from what was about to be the scene of the crime.

"So how do we save Baz?" Theo asked. "We have no idea when the fire will happen."

I looked up at the windows in the turrets. No lights were on. Nobody was home.

"Let's go see if he's in his tent," I said.

We left the castle and walked quickly to the end of the midway. I had to constantly push Lu to keep her moving. She was just as amazed to see the park in 1937 as Theo and I had been, and she kept stopping to take it all in.

"So cool," she kept saying, over and over.

When we finally arrived at Baz's orange-and-white tent, it was buzzing with activity.

"There's a show going on," I said. "I want to see this."

We hurried straight inside to find the place packed.

Baz really was a big attraction. It was standing room only. With every bench filled, we had to stand in the back along with a bunch of other people who had gotten there too late to find a seat.

Weird flute music was playing as Baz sat on his throne, staring into his crystal ball. There was one spotlight on him, making the scene all sorts of dramatic. The only other light was the glow that came from the crystal ball.

"Mallory Loehr!" Baz called out, his voice booming through the big tent.

A woman standing close to us gasped and shot a look at the guy next to her, not sure of what to do. Her eyes were wide. The guy laughed and nudged her forward.

"Here!" she yelled. "I'm back here!"

"You have an uncle who is quite ill," Baz exclaimed. "I am afraid his time is short."

The woman sighed and said, "I know. He's elderly. Been sick a long time now. His passing will be a blessing."

"It will be more than a blessing," Baz announced. "He is quite wealthy, and you are his sole heir. Congratulations, Mallory. You are about to become a very rich woman."

Mallory took a step back as if the announcement had physically hit her. I don't know if the news made her happy or sad. The audience reacted strangely. Some applauded. Some muttered with discomfort. It was a classic good news–bad news deal.

"Uh, are you sure?" Mallory called out.

Baz shot a dark, penetrating look her way. "About his passing or your good fortune?" he asked.

"Uh, both, I guess," Mallory said. She looked a little embarrassed to be asking about money, considering where it would come from.

"Why are you here if you doubt my ability?" Baz said with a sneer.

The woman was totally flustered. "I'm not—I mean—I don't . . . I mean, thank you. I think."

She didn't seem to know whether to laugh or cry. Her husband gave her a hug. I'll bet he mostly cared about the getting-rich part.

As I watched her, my eye caught someone I recognized in the audience. It was Mrs. Simmons, the wife of the pirate ship guy who Baz had predicted would die. She didn't look any better than the last time we'd seen her. She stood leaning against one of the thick tent poles, hugging her arms around her waist. While everyone else in the audience was whispering to one another with excitement about the prediction Baz had just made, Mrs. Simmons had her eyes locked on the oracle. Why was she there? It must have been torture for her to watch Baz make more predictions, especially about somebody who was going to die soon.

Baz threw up his hands to quiet the crowd.

The place instantly went silent. If anybody was breathing, I couldn't hear it.

When Baz raised his arms, he winced in pain and grabbed at his side.

A murmur of curiosity rippled through the crowd. Was this part of the act?

"What's his problem?" Lu whispered.

Baz steeled himself and raised his arms again, slower this time. He cringed but didn't give in and kept his arms held high.

The crowd went quiet again.

The flute music was all that could be heard. It was totally eerie.

Baz stood there for a long couple of seconds. Anticipation was building. Something was about to happen.

The crystal ball glowed brighter. Baz looked down at it with an expression that I can best describe as stunned. Whatever he was seeing in that crystal ball shocked him. That was strange, because this guy didn't get rattled. Even when he was facing an angry guy who wanted to skewer him with a sword, he didn't break a sweat. He stared into the light for a few seconds, then shouted, "The show is over!"

The effort of yelling triggered the pain in his side again. He clutched himself but didn't budge from the spot.

"Go!" he commanded. "Make your way to the exits."

Nobody was sure of what to do. They looked at one another questioningly, wondering if this might be part of the show.

It wasn't.

"Get out!" Baz screamed.

People got the hint. Or the command. There was a lot of grumbling as they slowly stood up and shuffled out.

We moved to the side, letting them pass. Nobody was happy. They all felt like they had been cheated out of a full show.

Mrs. Simmons didn't move. She stayed in place, gazing at Baz with a look that seemed like worry.

Baz continued to stare into the crystal ball, as if hypnotized by whatever he was seeing. The music ended and the houselights came on. Still, Baz didn't move.

"What's up with him?" Lu asked.

The three of us skirted around the crowd, moving against the flow, and made our way to the stage.

"What is he seeing?" Lu whispered.

"Whatever it is, he doesn't like it," Theo replied.

"I can guess what it is," I said. "Maybe Baz is a better oracle than we gave him credit for."

"Meaning . . . ?" Lu asked.

We were only a few yards away from Baz when a man came hurrying toward him across the stage. It was Hensley, the park manager.

"What the hell are you doing?" he yelled angrily. "Those are paying customers. You can't cut a show short!"

Hensley charged forward as if to tackle Baz, but Baz threw up his hand, making the other man stop short. It was like Baz had thrown out an invisible force field.

"Why am I seeing you again?" Baz asked through gritted teeth. For whatever reason, he was in a lot of pain. "Did I not make myself clear?"

"I ain't afraid of you, swami," Hensley said. "You understand? You can't touch me. I have more friends here than you do. Remember that."

Baz never took his eyes from the crystal ball. He didn't lower his hand either, or say another word to Hensley.

"Be smart," Hensley said. "Go home and figure out what your next move is. Think long and hard about it and get back here tomorrow for your shows. Your *full* shows. Understand?"

If Baz understood, he didn't say so.

Hensley turned and stormed off. The last person left in the tent besides us was Mrs. Simmons. She gave Baz one last worried look, then left.

Theo tugged on my arm to get me to leave, but there was no way. We were there to save Baz, whether he liked it or not.

The tent was now empty. I took a cautious step closer to the oracle and said, "You're seeing your own future, aren't you?"

Lu gasped with surprise.

"Of course!" Theo exclaimed.

Baz finally tore his gaze from the crystal ball. Instantly, the light that came from within went dark. When he looked at me, I saw the fear in his eyes.

"It's a fire, isn't it?" I asked. "That's what you saw."

Baz opened his mouth as if to say something, but no words came out.

"Please say you can change your future," Theo said.

I think Baz was in shock. He tried to say something, but all he could do was shake his head.

"You can!" Lu exclaimed. "Just stay away from your apartment."

Baz's eyes went unfocused. He glanced down at the crystal ball as if hoping it would show him something more. It didn't. The glass orb stayed dark. Suddenly, Baz ran off backstage, his purple robes billowing behind him.

"This is good, right?" Lu said, hopeful. "Now he can save himself."

"Did that look like somebody who thought everything was going to be okay?" Theo asked.

"Stop being so negative!" Lu exclaimed.

I took a step closer to the edge of the stage, where I got a good view of the crystal ball. I looked deep into the glass, hoping to see any hint of a vision that would predict the future.

"So where's the real power?" I asked my friends. "Is it Baz? Or the crystal ball?"

I didn't expect to see anything, but I did. It was like a fire burning within the glass. It was quick but unmistakable, and so real I imagined that I felt heat on my face.

"Whoa!" I exclaimed, and backed off. "Did you see that?"

"See what?" Lu asked.

"You didn't see the fire inside the crystal ball?"

Lu shook her head. I turned to Theo. Theo shrugged. Neither had seen it.

"I swear I saw something," I said.

"So what does that mean?" Lu asked.

"It means we've got to make sure Baz doesn't go home," I said.

I took off running for the exit with the others right behind me. We blasted out of the tent, only to get caught in the crowd of people who had just left Baz's show. There was no way to know if the fire was going to start right away, or later that night, or long after the park closed, but we couldn't take the chance. Baz was headed for trouble, and we had to make sure he didn't find it.

We had to prove that his predictions didn't have to come true.

We had to change the future.

We pushed our way through the crowd, taking way longer than we should have. Once we broke out from the masses, we jogged toward the midway.

"What are we going to do?" Lu asked, breathless.

"We keep Baz from going to his apartment," I answered.

"How?" Theo asked. "That guy doesn't listen to anybody."

"Then we'll drag him out," I said. "Or we'll go to that Hensley guy and tell him his Magic Castle ride is going to catch fire. Maybe he'll close it down."

"Or maybe closing it down is the exact thing that leads to the fire," Theo said.

I didn't want to think that. I had to believe we could change what was coming, because we knew what it was.

We ran onto the midway to discover that it was really crowded. There were so many people, it took forever for us to push our way through to the Magic Castle ride.

"I guess we don't have to worry about closing the ride," Lu said. "Look."

There was a sawhorse in front of the castle entrance with a bright yellow *Ride Closed* sign on it.

"It's already closed," Lu added.

"Uh-oh," Theo said, pointing up to the turret.

A light shone from a lone window high above. Baz was home.

"We'll go to Hensley," I said. "We'll get him to pull Baz out of there and—"

"Marcus!" Theo shouted.

"Theo, stop arguing!" Lu said, frustrated.

"I'm not arguing," Theo said. "I know how the fire started."

Lu and I shot him surprised looks.

"You do?" I exclaimed.

"Yeah. You were right. It wasn't an accident. It was set," Theo said, sounding numb. "Not by one of Baz's enemies either."

"Then who?" Lu asked.

"Look," Theo said, pointing toward the ride.

A lone person approached the entrance, but not on the pathway leading in. The person crept along the base of the ride in front of the bushes that surrounded the castle, as if trying to make sure nobody noticed him. In one hand he held something that he shielded with the other.

It was a lit candle.

He slipped in behind the *Ride Closed* sign and walked straight for the front door.

"He's afraid of the dark," Theo said. "So he's bringing in his own light."

It was Derby.

The kid glanced over his shoulder to see if he was being watched, then ducked inside the entrance and disappeared.

We'd found our fire starter.

CHAPTER
9

The three of us made our way through the crowded midway to get to the Magic Castle ride. I didn't even want to think why Derby would set fire to the place. It couldn't be because he was angry at the guys who were bullying him. That would be, like, psycho. It would have to be an accident.

An accident we had to prevent.

By the time we made it over the drawbridge and up to the ride's entrance, Derby had already been inside for a while. All we could do was try to catch up.

"Theo, go find Hensley," I said. "If we don't get there in time, he should call the fire department."

"Where do I look?" Theo said nervously, tugging on his ear.

"I have no idea," I exclaimed. "You're the smart one—figure it out."

"Right," Theo said, and jogged away.

"I hate dark rides," Lu said, staring at the ominous entrance.

"Me too," I said. "Let's make sure it *stays* dark." I grabbed her hand and pulled her inside.

The place was dark. I mean *pitch* dark. We couldn't see a thing and waited a few seconds for our eyes to adjust. Didn't help. It was still dead dark.

"No wonder Derby's afraid," Lu said, her voice wavering. "This is ridiculously creepy."

"We'll shuffle ahead slowly," I said.

I inched forward and walked straight into a wall.

"Ow!" I screamed. "What the heck? This is supposed to be fun?"

I put my hand out to feel my way along and kept moving ahead through the narrow corridor. It was slow going because I had to slide my hand across the wall or risk getting slammed again.

Lu said, "Whoever thought of this stupid ride was a demented—"

Honk!

A loud horn sounded next to us as a light came on to reveal the Frankenstein monster to our right. We could see a display through a window covered in chicken wire.

It was filled with tombstones, electrical laboratory giz-mos, and the monster himself. He lifted his arms and let out a groan. It was silly except for the surprise, which almost made me pee my pants. Lu pushed herself against me out of pure shock.

"Well, that sucked," she said.

We hurried past the dumb display and the light went out, waiting to surprise the next innocent victim.

"There must be a trigger in the floor," I said. "When somebody steps on it, boom, surprise."

The display was hokey, but not knowing when the next scare was going to pop out made the whole deal nerve-racking.

We moved on slowly, and a few seconds later . . .

Wheeeee!

A shrill whistle blew as the next display lit up. It was Dracula sitting up in his coffin. This dummy was pretty cheesy, too, and not scary at all. It was all about the surprise.

"I hate this," Lu said.

"Derby!" I called out.

No answer.

"He had a candle to help him see where to go," Lu said. "He could move a lot faster."

We turned a corner and entered a room that was fully lit. It was painted with vertical orange and purple stripes, which made it look like a circus tent. It wasn't until we stepped into the room that the purpose of the stripes was clear. The floor was tilted on a forty-five-degree angle. The stripes gave the optical illusion that it was level. We had to walk through a maze of handrails, snaking back and forth, hanging on for fear of falling down.

"Is this supposed to be fun?" Lu asked as she slammed into one handrail.

There was nothing even close to enjoyable about this demented spook house.

Beyond the slanted room were more dark corridors. After a few turns we reached a passageway that was lit up, but the floor was covered with spinning disks that made it nearly impossible to cross over without falling down.

"This is, like, dangerous," Lu said. "We could twist an ankle. They'd never have this kind of stuff nowadays."

I kept hoping we'd run into Derby after every turn.

"Where would he start the fire?" I asked. "I hope he didn't know about some hidden service door that we missed."

We passed through a maze of glass just like the one in the Hall of Mirrors. Thankfully, I didn't see any floating shadows. The maze was followed by a room with a row of distorting mirrors. As we kept moving forward, each new room was connected by more dark, maddening corridors filled with pop-up scares.

"This can't go on much longer," Lu said. "We've gotta come out the other side eventually."

"Listen," I said.

Somebody was up ahead. The voices were muffled, but it sounded like there was more than one person, and they were arguing.

"Got him," I said, grabbing Lu's hand.

We hurried through the next dark corridor, ignoring the creepy circus clown and the werewolf that jumped out at us. With each step we took, the sounds of the scuffle got louder. Finally, we broke out of the dark corridor into a large room that looked like a dense forest. From the ceiling hung dozens of green streamers that appeared to be made of thick cotton or burlap. It was like pushing through a sea of heavy, dangling spaghetti.

More important, this was the room where the voices were coming from. It sounded as though a fight was going on between kids. Some cheered as the sounds of the fight grew louder.

"Hey!" I shouted.

The fight stopped.

"Somebody's coming!" one kid yelled.

"Go!"

"Scram!"

"No scramming!" I yelled. "Don't move!"

The sound of footsteps running away was obvious.

"Do you smell that?" Lu asked.

I took a whiff. Yup, something was burning. I pushed forward, throwing aside the hanging strands, desperate to find the source.

"There's smoke!" Lu yelled.

Wispy smoke drifted between the draped tendrils. We were getting closer. I followed my nose as much as anything else, and when I pushed aside one hanging vine, I saw it.

Flames were licking up the length of one of the vines, spreading toward the ceiling and the forest of other vines that dangled beside it, waiting to ignite. I quickly whipped off my sweater and used it to smother the flames. Another couple of minutes and the fire would have spread like crazy.

We had gotten there just in time.

Lu bent down and picked up a candle from the floor directly beneath the vine that had been on fire.

"He really did try to torch the place," she said. "Why would he do that? And who were the other kids? He came in here alone."

"No idea," I said. "But you know what? Who cares? We stopped the fire. We changed the story. Baz's predictions don't have to come true."

"We can save Theo," Lu added with a big smile. "I knew it."

We hurried the rest of the way through the ride and exited onto the midway, where Theo was waiting with Mr. Hensley.

Hensley looked pissed.

"What happened?" Theo asked.

"False alarm," I said, and handed the candle to Hensley. "Somebody dropped this inside by accident."

Hensley took the candle and looked at it like it was an alien artifact. "Somebody brought a candle in there?" he asked, stunned. "What kind of fool would do that?"

I wasn't going to tell him. It was none of my business. This wasn't Derby's story; it was Baz's.

"I don't know," I said. "But we snuffed out a fire before it could spread. You might want to check it out."

Hensley left us and headed for the castle without a word. His mind must have been racing ahead to the fact that Playland had just dodged another disaster bullet.

Theo looked at us hopefully.

"You put it out?" he asked. "There's no fire?"

With a big smile Lu said, "We really do have control over our lives."

Theo laughed giddily. "That's great! I'm not doomed!"

"I told you!" Lu exclaimed.

"Let's not celebrate just yet," I said. "All we proved

is that Baz's predictions don't have to come true. We still have to figure out what's waiting for Theo on his birthday."

Theo's smile dropped.

"Oh. Right," he said, suddenly depressed again. "Well, that was fun while it lasted."

"It's okay," I said. "I've got an idea of how we can do that."

"How?" Lu asked, incredulous. "Now *you* can see the future?"

"Maybe," I replied. "Let's go."

A few minutes later we were back in Baz's tent. The place was eerily empty.

"I think this whole fortune-telling thing isn't just about Baz," I said. "I swear I saw something in that crystal ball, and I'm no oracle."

We all stepped up onto the stage and approached the crystal ball, which sat on a purple velvet pillow.

"I think it's all about this thing," I said. "This is the exact same crystal ball they're going to put in the fortune-telling machine."

Theo brightened and said, "Yes! That would explain why the machine can see into the future. Baz is gone, but the crystal ball still works."

"Touch it, Theo," I said.

"What? Really?"

"Yeah. It's like the thing senses when there's something to tell. This is about your future, so introduce yourself."

Theo looked at the glass ball like it was alive, and who knows? Maybe it was. He reached out slowly, his fingers getting closer and closer to the orb.

"Boo!" Lu whispered in Theo's ear.

Theo yelped and jumped backward as if Lu had screamed at him.

Lu couldn't help but giggle. "I'm sorry, that was cheap."

"Don't kid around!" Theo scolded. "This is about your cousin too."

"I know, I know," Lu said, trying to keep from smiling. "Go ahead."

Theo reached out again, more tentatively than before. He gave a warning glance to Lu, making sure she wouldn't mess with him again.

Lu winked at him.

Theo's fingers got closer. Slowly.

"I don't think it'll hurt you," I said.

"I'm not worried about it hurting me," Theo replied. "I'm worried about what it might show me."

He took a breath, braced himself, and touched the crystal.

Nothing happened.

He reached out and touched it again.

Nothing.

He put his hand on top like he was palming a basketball.

Nada.

Theo took a step back, the tension gone.

"Maybe it *is* about Baz," he said. "He might have the power to trigger this thing."

At that exact instant there was a flash within the glass ball. It was fast. If I'd blinked, I would have missed it. It was like a movie was being projected inside. I saw a violent image that looked like a crash. Some kind of vehicle hit a hard surface and crumbled. There was no sound, only a fleeting image. I couldn't make out any more than what looked like a panel of red metal that crumbled on contact. There was water too. Spraying water. I saw a flash of a person. It was a guy. A black guy. He was wearing a bright blue shirt. It was so fast that I couldn't tell if it was Theo or not. I also saw a brief flash of a white guy who looked like he had orange hair. That was the weirdest image of all, but it only added to the bizarre burst of random visuals.

"Whoa!" I shouted.

"I saw it!" Theo exclaimed.

"I did too," Lu added. "It looked like a crash."

"Oh man," Theo whined. "Was that me? I've got a

blue shirt like that. Am I going to die in a crash? Why can't we see more?"

He knelt down and looked into the ball, but the show was over.

"How can Baz make such specific predictions if all he sees are quick flashes of things?" Theo asked.

"Maybe that's where the oracle part comes in," I said. "Maybe he sees more. Or he knows how to put the images together to make sense."

"We need him here," Lu said. "We saved his life. He owes us."

She was about to jump off the stage when the sound of a siren tore through the night.

"Now what?" Lu exclaimed.

The siren got louder. It was coming closer.

"Sounds like a fire truck," Theo said. "You don't suppose—"

I didn't wait for him to finish his thought. I jumped off the stage and sprinted for the exit. The park wasn't as busy as before. There was nobody to stand in our way as we ran back to the midway. We soon discovered why. People had left the rest of the park and gathered on the midway to watch the spectacle.

When we saw what they were all staring at, my stomach fell.

The Magic Castle was on fire.

Fire licked out from every window, sending choking black smoke into the night sky. It seemed as though it had started low and shot straight up the central structure that supported the main turret.

The turret that held Baz's apartment.

The ride was done for, and so was Baz.

We stood on the edge of the crowd, gazing up at the inferno in stunned wonder.

"I thought you put the fire out!" Theo exclaimed.

"I did! I swear."

"He did," Lu said with certainty. "It was definitely out."

Theo sighed and said, "So then, we were wrong. No matter what we do, we can't change the future."

Watching the ride go up in flames was too depressing for all sorts of reasons. There was nothing left for us to do in the story, so we trudged back toward the maintenance workshop in the carousel building. None of us said anything about what it all meant. Mostly because I don't think anybody knew. I used the Paradox key on the closet door, and we were soon back in the Library.

We found Everett at his usual spot, reading the latest developments in the black book that contained the story of the Oracle Baz. The three of us stood there, staring at Everett, hoping he could offer some kind of wisdom or insight as to what had gone wrong.

All he said was, "Are you absolutely sure you put out the fire?"

"Yes!" I exclaimed in frustration. "I don't know how much more *out* it could be. But even if I missed a little ember, there's no way it would have spread so quickly. That place was like an inferno!"

"It spread because it had to," Theo said with no emotion. "Call it fate or destiny or whatever you want, but it's too powerful to be changed. The future is like a magnet that keeps pulling us in the direction it wants us to go. All we did in that story was prove it."

"No!" Lu exclaimed. "Nothing controls my future but me. I decide what's going to happen."

"I don't think anybody has total control over what happens to them," I said.

"I know that," she shot back. "But the future isn't written yet, no matter what shadows pop up in a stupid crystal ball. We may not be able to change what happened in the past, but we sure as heck can change what hasn't happened yet."

"I wish you were right," Theo said. "But everything I've seen says you aren't."

"Then give up," Lu said angrily. "Let whatever's going to happen, happen. I can't do that. I won't. I'm not going down without a fight."

Lu stormed off, headed for the door that would lead back to my bedroom.

The rest of us looked at one another, unsure of what to say.

"What do you think, Everett?" I asked. "Is the future set in stone?"

Everett closed the book and tossed it onto the circulation desk.

"I wish I could be of more help," he said. "I exist in a very different world from the one you all live in. The lives of the spirits that haunt these books are fluid. When you enter stories that took place in the past, you're stepping into a memory. We can help the spirits understand the dilemmas they encountered, but it doesn't change what actually happened to them when they were alive."

"But we did change the future," I said. "The actual future. We shut down the Black Moon Circle and captured the Boggin."

"Aye," Everett said. "Because that was reality. You didn't change the past; you influenced real events that hadn't happened yet."

"Exactly!" I exclaimed. "That's what we're trying to do here!"

"Indeed," Everett said. "The difference here is you were given a glimpse of the future. Of events that have yet to happen. I can't tell you how Baz is able to do that, or why that crystal ball offers that window, but from everything I've read, the power is real. And accurate."

"But can the future be changed?" I asked.

"I truly don't know," he said with a sigh. "I'm sorry."

"Not as sorry as I am," Theo said. "I'm going home."

He took off, headed back to reality, leaving Everett and me alone.

"So here's the question," Everett said. "How can this be fixed? Is it about going back into the story to figure out what the disruption was? Or is it better to stay in reality and do what you can to avoid disaster?"

"Maybe I can do both," I said.

An idea was forming. I didn't know exactly how I would make it happen, but at least it was an idea.

"Both?" Everett said.

I grabbed the book and flipped through pages, my excitement growing.

"There was something that happened," I said. "I don't remember the exact words but . . . here!"

I found the section of the story that had been tickling at my imagination since I first read it.

———————

BAZ STARED DEEP INTO the crystal and scowled. "You are employed here at the park?" he asked.

"I'm on break," Simmons replied. "It's allowed."

"Go home," Baz snapped. "Do not return to your duties today."

"I said, it's allowed," Simmons said, annoyed. "I can come to the shows."

"I don't care what your superiors have authorized you to do," Baz snarled. "If you remain here at the park, your life will be in grave danger."

I closed the book and said, "Baz saw that guy's future. He saw that Simmons was going to die and told him to leave the park."

Everett sat up straight; his hope was growing along with mine.

"Baz tried to save the man," he said. "Does that mean it was possible?"

"I don't know, but why would he warn Simmons if he didn't think the future could be changed?"

"I believe you're right, lad!" Everett exclaimed. "But we don't have the same advantage. Baz saw what Simmons was in for. We don't know where Lu's cousin disappeared to or what fate awaits Theo."

"But we came close," I said. "When Theo touched that crystal ball, we saw images. There was a crash. And twisted metal. And all sorts of stuff that wasn't too pretty."

"That isn't much of a help," Everett said.

"No, we need to know more. We *have* to know more."

I went toward the door, headed for home.

"How do you propose to do that?" Everett asked.

"Easy," I replied. "I'm going to steal a crystal ball."

CHAPTER
10

It was Friday evening.

Two days before Theo's birthday, when, according to his fortune, life as he knew it would end.

Though Theo's dilemma was more pressing, Annabella Lu didn't lose sight of the fact that her cousin Jenny's disappearance was also very much a part of the story. Rather than returning to her home after leaving the Library, Lu paid another visit to her aunt Tina's house.

"Is it okay if I spend the night in Jenny's room?" Lu asked her aunt.

"Of course, child, but why?"

Lu shrugged and said, "I don't know. I'm just

trying to do all I can to figure out what happened to her. You never know–maybe I'll get inspired."

Aunt Tina gave her a loving and grateful hug, though she had no real hope that having her favorite niece sleep in her missing daughter's room would solve any mysteries. Still, she gave Lu a kiss and wished her a good night.

Lu shut herself in Jenny's room. Though she was exhausted, she couldn't sleep. After tossing in bed for over an hour, she gave up trying, got out of bed, and sat at Jenny's desk. For the one hundredth time, she read the fortune card Jenny had been given by the machine that held the fortune-telling crystal ball of the Oracle Baz.

SEIZE THE MOMENT. YOU MAY NOT GET ANOTHER OPPORTUNITY. FOLLOW YOUR HEART.

What could it mean?

What had the crystal ball seen in Jenny's future? Did it have anything to do with her disappearance?

With only the narrow shaft of light from the lamp shining on Jenny's desk, Lu slowly scanned the collection of odds and ends that helped define her cousin's life and history. There was a Hello Kitty notepad; a

Tower of Terror mug filled with pens and pencils; multiple hair clips in every color; framed photos of Jenny with her parents; a jewelry box; half a dozen stuffed animals with oversized eyes; a stack of well-read books; a princess brush that Jenny had used since she was a toddler; the box from her iPhone; an array of makeup tubes and jars that were neatly arranged like a line of soldiers; a . . .

Wait.

The box from her iPhone.

Lu sat bolt upright, even more awake than before.

She grabbed the box and pulled it open to find . . . nothing. No phone. Only a receipt. Lu pulled it out, checked the date, and smiled.

She dropped the box and the receipt and started going through the desk drawers, quickly digging in each one. She was on a mission for she knew exactly what to look for. In the third drawer she found it.

Jenny's old iPhone. Not the new one that had come in the box.

Lu plugged the phone into the power cord that ran up from the wall outlet and waited for it to power up.

"Come on . . . come on," Lu implored impatiently.

Finally, Jenny's home screen appeared. There

was no lock screen and request for a passcode. Jenny didn't bother with security. The home screen was a picture of her two cats, Abbie and Winston. The picture made Lu smile for a second, but no more than that. Her mind was racing too far ahead.

She went right to the phone icon and opened up the recent calls Jenny had made and received. Though "recent" was only as recent as the moment when Jenny activated her new phone and deactivated the old one. The date on the receipt confirmed Lu's memory: Jenny had gotten the new phone shortly before she went missing. Until then she had been using the phone that Lu now held in her hands.

A list of numbers appeared, both from incoming and outgoing calls. Lu recognized only a few numbers that belonged to their family. Her own number was there a few times too. Those didn't interest her. But there was another number that did. It had a Connecticut area code, which wasn't unusual. The odd thing was that it showed up dozens of times. Multiple dozens. Whoever belonged to that number, Jenny had spoken to them again and again right before she disappeared. The name associated with the number was simply "Jo."

It took only a few seconds for Lu to skim through Jenny's contact list to find "Jo." The contact picture showed a pretty girl with Asian features who flashed a two-fingered peace sign.

Lu was focused and on fire. She turned on Jenny's old-school tower computer. It took what felt like an eternity to boot up as Lu sat there, nervously drumming her fingers on the desk. The whole while she kept staring at the smiling face of Jo on Jenny's phone. Lu didn't know Jo and didn't remember Jenny ever talking about her. But from the number of times they had talked with one another recently, it sure seemed as though her cousin knew Jo pretty well.

Once the computer had booted up, Lu started Firefox and went straight to Facebook. In seconds she was on Jenny's page and searching through her friends list. Jenny had more than a few friends. A few hundred was more like it. Lu had to force herself to slow down and focus on each tiny profile picture. She didn't want to miss any.

When she was getting near the end of the list and beginning to fear she had struck out, she found it.

Jo Wong.

It was the exact same picture that Jenny had on her phone.

Lu's heart raced and her hand trembled as she clicked on Jo's name. Now that she was so close, she feared that her efforts might lead to nothing. Her ten minutes of excitement and hope could come to an abrupt and disappointing dead end. After what felt like half a lifetime, Jo Wong's page appeared.

Lu scrolled down, examining Jo's posts . . .

. . . and let out a yelp.

"Gotcha!" she yelled.

Lu jumped up, ran out of Jenny's room, and sprinted along the upstairs hallway.

It was past midnight. Her aunt and uncle would surely be asleep.

Lu didn't care. She burst into their room and leapt onto the bed.

"Wha–?" Uncle Nathan shouted, dazed.

Aunt Tina let out a yelp of surprise.

"It's okay, it's me," Lu announced.

"Annabella?" Aunt Tina said, still half-asleep and more than a little confused.

"What are you doing?" Uncle Nathan asked.

"Wrong question," Lu said, barely containing her excitement. "It's not what I'm *doing*–it's what I *did*."

"What did you do?" Aunt Tina asked.

"I found Jenny."

———

CHAPTER

11

Saturday morning.

T minus one day to Theo's birthday.

The day I would become a criminal.

I didn't really plan on stealing Baz's crystal ball. Not really. It was more like a loan. I just wanted to borrow it long enough to get the information I needed to save my friend's life. I fully expected to return it. But it wasn't like I could explain that to the people at Playland and expect them to say, *Why, sure, young fella! Go right ahead! Take the antique crystal ball and see if you can change the future. Good luck to you!*

That wouldn't happen, which is why I found myself on the bus and headed for Playland at the silly hour of six o'clock. I doubted that the guard Eugene would be up and patrolling that early. I mean, who breaks into an amusement park at that hour? Nobody. Nobody but me, that is. My plan was to be in, out, and back on the bus with the crystal ball before anybody realized what had happened. Heck, I might get it back before they even realized it was gone. That ancient arcade barely had any visitors even when the park was open.

But returning the crystal ball was the least of my worries. I needed to get it home, put it in front of Theo, and hope it really did have the power to give us a clue to what might happen the next day. That was all that mattered.

I was the only one on the bus when the driver let me out at the end of Playland Parkway. It was the same driver who had dropped me off before, and he gave me the same curious look.

"I know it's closed," I said to the guy.

The driver just shrugged and drove off. He didn't care.

Dawn wouldn't come until six-thirty, which meant the park was in early-morning twilight. Perfect. I could hug the buildings of the midway and blend in, unnoticed, like a stealth fighter. Without sunlight, the normally bright colors of the park were muted and gray, giving it the look of a faded black-and-white picture. It only added to the feeling of eerie emptiness. As I moved quickly along, I couldn't help but think of the many tragic events that had happened at the park. Was this place cursed? Had it been built over an ancient burial ground? Or was it just the victim of some incredibly bad luck?

When I slid past the Hall of Mirrors, a chill went up my spine, but I stayed focused and kept moving. I was amped up enough. I didn't need to start imagining what had been in there with me.

I had to cross the midway and the grassy strip that ran in the center of it to get to the bumper car ride. This was where Eugene had spotted me the last time, so instead of moving in a straight line, I ran from tree to tree, shielding myself as best as I could.

Speed was everything. The longer I was there, the better the chances were that I would get caught. I jumped the chest-high wall that enclosed the bumper cars to take a shortcut through the track itself. I hurried across the empty expanse to the ride's exit on the far side, and the sidewalk that would lead to the arcade. So far so good. No whistles were blown. No alarms went off. I had made it.

But the second I stepped inside the arcade, I was hit with an overpowering sense of . . . what? I wasn't scared. Or creeped out. It was more like an intense sadness. It was still pretty dark, so the games were little more than silhouettes. Being surrounded by those antique ma-chines made me feel as though I had stepped back in time. Again. There was nothing in there that had been built in the past fifty years. The park had a lot of history, and not all of it was good.

I walked slowly along one aisle, surrounded by the past. Unlike modern arcade games that were all about LED lights and music and animation, these things were made of wood and metal. They were mechanical. Their artwork showed laughing clowns and happy kid faces and cowboys and animals that were all from another era. Whoever had made these machines was long gone. It was like walking among mechanical ghosts. I couldn't help but feel as though a hundred pairs of eyes were on me, silently questioning why I had dared to enter their forgotten little universe.

That feeling intensified about a thousand times when I rounded the end of one aisle and caught sight of the glass box that held the Oracle Baz. Or his dummy, looking as though he was sitting inside a glass coffin. At least his eyes were focused on the crystal ball, not me.

The crystal ball. That's what I had come for.

I hurried along the aisle of games until I stood face to face with Baz. Or face to dummy. He was the dummy. I think. Even though the life-sized mannequin was eerily like the real thing, complete with his superior sneer, once I got that close I was way more interested in the crystal ball.

It sat on a purple velvet pillow and looked no different from an ordinary globe of glass. Did this thing really have the power to predict the future? It sure seemed so, though I didn't buy into Theo's atomic-power theory. As hard as it was to stop logic from taking over and thinking there was no way a hunk of glass could possess that kind of magic, I had to hope it did. Theo's life depended on it.

I reached up and ran my fingers along the edge of the wooden cabinet, searching for a hinge or a latch or anything that would show me how to open it. This was a machine. Machines needed service. There had to be a way to get in. The good news: I felt hinges along the left edge. The bad news: instead of a latch on the opposite side, there was a series of screws. My heart sank. This was going to take some time. At least I had come prepared. I reached into my hoodie and pulled out a Phillips screwdriver that I had grabbed from my father's workshop. Sometimes I can be smart like that. I got right to work, figuring that I not only had to unscrew a bunch of screws but also would have to screw them back in after grabbing the crystal ball. With any luck, nobody would notice that the ball was gone, and I'd return it as soon as I could.

I didn't stop to think or question that I was doing something idiotic. And totally illegal. I just got to work.

As soon as I started to unscrew the first screw, I heard a strange noise. It sounded like a gentle thump. It wasn't scary or anything. It was just out of place. I stopped working and listened. A few seconds passed and I was about to get back to work when I heard several more thumps. It sounded like something was rolling around and banging into things. My curiosity got the better of me, and I followed the sound.

The mystery didn't last long. It was a pinball machine. The metal pinball was moving inside the game, but since the power wasn't turned on, the only sound it made was from the ball bouncing against the bumpers. A few seconds later the ball reached the bottom and disappeared into the hole that sent it to the chute that would line it up for the next shot.

There was nothing weird about it except that it had happened. It wasn't like somebody was playing the game. How had the ball been released? I figured it had probably been stuck there for a while and finally fell free. Maybe I had jostled it when I ran by. Whatever the reason, it was done, so I turned back toward Baz's machine.

And another ball released.

I spun around quickly to see the exact same thing happen. The metal ball rolled through the game, bouncing off bumpers. There was no reason for that to have happened. At least none that made sense. But I couldn't stress over it. Time was ticking.

I ran back to Baz's machine and worked quickly to unscrew the next screw.

That's when I heard another thump.

This one was much louder than the others, and it had enough power behind it to make the wall shake. This was no small pinball. There was something on the other side of the wall. Something big.

Thump!

It happened again. Somebody or some*thing* was on the other side, banging against the wall. I tried to ignore it but couldn't. I had to know what it was. So I ran out of the arcade the way I had come and headed around the corner toward the bumper car track.

On the far side of the track, a bumper car was moving. There was no power on, but the little red car didn't know that. Nobody was behind the wheel either. At least I'd solved the mystery of what was doing the bumping. The red car moved forward, thumped against the barricade that ringed the track, and was sent backward. It then hit the car behind it, which sent it moving forward, where it hit the barricade again.

I stood on the track, watching this dance go on and on. I must have gone into brain lock, because I couldn't come up with any explanation for why this was happening. I was so mesmerized that I let the screwdriver drop out of my hand. It fell onto the track and made a loud clatter that echoed through the cavernous structure.

The bumper car stopped instantly. It was as if the sound had broken whatever cycle it was stuck in. I didn't move for fear it would start up again.

And it did. The car inched forward toward the barricade. But this time it didn't hit. It turned. The little red car with nobody at the wheel moved away from the spot it had been sandwiched in and continued to slide across the track . . . toward me!

I was like a deer caught in the headlights of an oncoming car. I stood with my back to the barrier that surrounded the track, unable to get my feet moving. The car picked up speed, cruising directly at me. It was like it knew I was there. My mind raced, trying to understand what was going on, but nothing came to me.

The car kept sliding closer with no sign of slowing down. It was seconds away from hitting me and pinning me against the track barrier. Once I realized what a bad spot I was in, I got moving. I snatched up the screwdriver, then quickly boosted myself up and over the barrier. A second later the red car drove into the wall right where I'd been standing. It hit with a solid thump and stopped right there.

I kept my eyes on it from the safety of the other side of the barrier, waiting for it to make its next move. I must have waited a full minute, but the car didn't budge. There was no explanation for what had happened, and I didn't really care. All I wanted was to be somewhere else. But I couldn't leave without the crystal ball. So as much as I was ready to run for the park's exit, instead I sprinted back along the path to the arcade to crack the machine open, grab the ball, and get the heck out of there.

I went right to work on the screws, desperate to get them out before anything else weird happened. My hands were shaking with nervous energy, and the screwdriver kept slipping out of the screw heads. By trying to go fast, I was taking far longer to get the job done than if I had just slowed down and stayed calm. But calm wasn't happening just then. I had gotten two screws out and had two more to go when I heard some kind of mechanical whirring.

The sound was coming from behind me. I didn't want to turn around. I didn't want to see what it was. I didn't want to be there anymore. But I had to look. I turned around slowly to see that one of the games across the aisle from the Baz machine had come to life. It was a big glass cube that held a two-foot-tall marionette.

A clown marionette.

I hate clowns. Whoever was the first person to think

it was a good idea to put on hideous makeup that makes your features bigger than life while wearing rainbow clothes was just plain demented. The clown doll hung from wires attached to its arms and legs, standing upright in all its clowny freakishness. The doll was lit from below by the glow of a row of bulbs that had sprung to life. Why was there suddenly power? The wheezy sound of circus calliope music began to play. I wasn't even worried about anybody hearing and coming to find out what was going on. I was too focused on the creepy little clown. I actually left the Baz machine and walked toward the marionette. It was like I was being drawn there. I don't know if I was moving closer to try and figure out how the machine could have turned itself on, or because that sinister little puppet was somehow hypnotizing me. Whatever the reason, I moved closer.

When I was only a step away, the clown's arm twitched.

And I jumped.

The idea of the machine was to put in your nickel and move the handles in front. That would make the clown's arms wave or his knees bend. You could make the thing dance, which might have been fun for a three-year-old . . . a hundred years ago.

It wasn't much fun for me, that was for sure, especially because I wasn't touching the controls. The clown hopped on one leg, which made its arms bounce. It jumped back and forth from one leg to the other in a macabre doll dance in time to the haunting calliope music.

I was losing my mind. Nobody was controlling this thing. The knobs in front weren't moving. I tried to tell myself that it was preprogrammed to do the lame dance, but that didn't explain why it had turned itself on. I couldn't take my eyes off of it. All thoughts of the crystal ball and Theo and the fact that I was trespassing had flown out of my head.

And then the clown stopped dancing. So did the music. I was left in eerie silence. I kept staring at the little freak, hoping the performance was over.

It wasn't. The doll's arms were at its sides. Slowly, one rose until it was parallel with the floor. Its little clown finger was pointing at something. There was no mistake. Its head was tilted to the side with a blank expression. Its dead eyes looked nowhere. But its finger was pointing as if telling me to look.

I didn't want to, but I had to. I turned slowly to see it was pointing at Baz's fortune-telling machine. I had no idea why . . .

. . . until Baz's machine came to life.

The lightbulbs inside his little cubicle warmed up, bathing the box in an eerie yellow glow. The lights created deep shadows under Baz's eyes, making the dumb dummy look more like a menacing dummy. Seeing the lights come on was a surprise. It wasn't the worst surprise.

Baz's arm moved.

The machine was gearing up to tell a fortune.

Nobody else was around. There was only one person there whose fortune it could tell.

Mine.

I didn't think for a second it was going to tell me I was about to win a million dollars. Every cell in my brain was screaming at me to get out of there. But I couldn't. I had to know.

Slowly, I walked back to the machine. Baz's lifeless eyes stared deep into the crystal ball as a blue light glowed from within it. Strange flute music drifted from the machine—the same kind of music that had played during Baz's live performance eighty years earlier. It was a pretty dramatic presentation, for an ancient machine.

One I didn't really care to see.

I walked right up to the machine. Baz's head behind the glass loomed above me. His arm made a mechanical sweeping motion over the crystal ball, and the blue light went out. His hand continued on to a box of cards that sat next to the crystal. The hand reached down and plucked out a card; the same kind of card that Theo and Jenny had gotten. The mechanical fingers clenched the card as the hand lifted and swiveled toward an opening in the table. The fingers opened and released the card. It dropped through the hole and appeared in a small trough in the front of the machine's cabinet, ready for the taking.

The lights went out and the music ended. Baz went back to staring into the dark crystal ball. The show was over.

But my fortune was sitting in front of me.

Reaching for it was like moving my hand through pudding. I knew I had to read it, but part of me was holding back, convinced I shouldn't. It was a battle being fought inside my brain. I truly feared what the card would say. I finally plucked it from the trough and looked at it. On one side was the familiar logo: *The Oracle Baz*. My fortune would be on the other side. My hand was shaking. Literally shaking. It took an incredible amount of willpower, but I finally turned the card over.

A single word was written on the card, printed in bold capital letters:

RUN!

Run? What did that mean? That wasn't a fortune. I kept staring at the card, trying to understand.

I looked up at the dummy of the Oracle Baz and nearly screamed.

Baz was looking straight at me. His eyes were focused with an intent gleam that made my heart stop.

That's when he spoke.

"Run!" the dummy said.

I got the message. I was outta there. I turned, ready to take off and sprint as far away from this cursed amusement park as I could get. But when I turned, I saw that I wasn't alone.

At the far end of the aisle of ancient games stood a shadow. Or what seemed to be a shadow. It was the shape of a man who stood there, blocking my way. Its outline was sharp and defined, as if it had been cut out of reality to leave a dark void. There was no detail inside, only eternal black.

The visitor from the Hall of Mirrors was back.

I put on the brakes and stood facing the apparition, too stunned to move.

The shadow lifted its arm, pulling the shadow of a curved sword from a sheath. There was no detail to the sword, but its outline was unmistakable.

The shadow lifted the sword over its head threateningly, ready to bring it down hard.

On me.

Another fortune was about to come true. My fortune.

I ran.

CHAPTER
12

The shadow, or whatever it was, blocked my way out of the arcade, so I turned and sprinted past Baz's machine, desperate to find another way out. I made it to the far end of the room, rounded another arcade machine, and came face to face with the shadow again. It stood only a few yards in front of me.

And it spoke.

"Thief!" it shouted.

At least I think it shouted. It wasn't like I saw its lips move or anything. Though it was definitely man-shaped, the thing was totally black. I couldn't see through it like a normal shadow. Normal? Normal shadows didn't yell at people. Or jump around and get in your way, for that matter. And it wasn't even a shadow, because there was nobody there to make a shadow.

Whatever it was, it moved toward me while raising the sword high.

Normal shadows don't do that either.

I did a one-eighty and ran in a third direction, sprinting past the rows of arcade games while glancing around for fear the shadow would pop up again and slice me. I skirted the perimeter of the big room until I saw the exit. It was only a few yards ahead. Once through that door, I wasn't going to stop running until I got to the bus stop. Or maybe I'd run all the way home. I definitely had enough energy for that. Only a few more steps and . . .

. . . the shadow stepped into the doorway to the outside, blocking the way.

I skidded to a stop. No amount of running was going to get me away from this thing, not if it could move around that fast.

"I wasn't going to steal the crystal ball," I shouted at it. "I just need it to—"

"Hey, who's in there?" I heard a voice call from outside.

The shadow vanished. It didn't fade or drift away like smoke. It simply blinked out like it was an image on TV and somebody cut the power.

"What's all the shouting?" the voice said again.

I was still too stunned to move, even after Eugene the security guard stepped into the doorway. Only a few minutes before, he was the last guy in the world I wanted to see, but at that moment I could have hugged him.

He scanned the arcade quickly, and when he focused on me, his shoulders dropped. I don't know if it was in relief or disappointment.

"You again?" he said with dismay.

He started toward me, walking quickly, as if ready to grab me by my shirt to heave me out of there.

"Did you see it?" I yelled. "It was a . . . a . . . shadow. With a sword!"

That stopped him cold.

"Say that again?" he said.

"It was right there," I said, my voice about three octaves higher than normal. I guess fear will do that. "It was a shadow. Or . . . or . . . not a shadow. It was like a negative-person. There was nothing but black where a normal person would be. And it talked. I think it's the thing I saw in the Hall of Mirrors. It was coming after me. With a sword! Did I mention that?"

I don't know why I said all that. It was like verbal diarrhea. It had to come out. There was no way Eugene would believe me. But I was too amped up to be cool about it. I stood there breathing hard, too terrified over what had happened to worry about what this security guard would do to me.

"There wasn't any shadow," Eugene said calmly.

"Yes, there was! I saw it! It talked to me!"

"It talked?" he asked.

"Yes! I wasn't imagining it."

Eugene looked all sorts of confused. Where a second ago it had seemed as though he was going to grab me and toss my butt out of there, he now looked concerned. Concern was good.

"I know you weren't imagining it," he said. "But it wasn't a shadow."

That threw me. Eugene believed me. Sort of.

"Then what was it?" I asked.

Eugene took off his cap and ran his hand through his gray hair, as though getting ready to confront a problem he was tired of dealing with. After a long sigh he said, "That, my young friend, was the Oracle Baz."

Eugene led me behind the Ye Olde Gold Mine ride to a kitchen that looked like it was used by the staff at Playland. Since it was November, nobody was there, unless you counted Eugene and the occasional sword-wielding ghost.

Eugene told me to make myself some hot chocolate,

so I used a teakettle to heat up water and tore open a pack of instant mix while he sat at a table quietly, watching me. I focused all my attention on the simple task of making the drink. I didn't really want it, but it kept my mind from spinning out of control and my hands from shaking. It felt like an entirely sane and normal thing to do because at that moment I was feeling anything but.

When I finished making the drink, I sat across from him. There was no more dodging the question. I had to know what was happening at Playland.

"So," I said, sounding totally casual. "The place is haunted."

Eugene raised his eyebrows in surprise, then burst out laughing. "Well, you're taking that news in stride," he said.

"I'm used to it," I said, deadly serious.

Eugene instantly stopped laughing and looked at me curiously. "Why did you come back? To help your friend? The one who got the bad fortune?"

"Yeah, but first tell me about Baz," I said. "That shadow thing is his ghost?"

Eugene chuckled. "I ain't crazy, if that's what you're thinking."

"Trust me, chief. I've seen way stranger things than that."

He gave me a curious look. "Have you, now?"

"Please just tell me about Baz," I said.

Eugene stood and strolled around the room, looking at the old black-and-white photos that hung on the walls. They showed Playland through the ages.

"I told you that Baz lived in a room over the Magic Castle ride."

He stopped at a vintage photo of the Magic Castle. I recognized the castle-like building, with its massive turrets. Eugene only knew it from pictures. I, on the other hand, had walked through it.

"The ride caught fire and Baz died," Eugene said. "Horrible way to go. Baz may have died that night, but people believe he never really left Playland. There are all sorts of stories about sightings. They've had paranormal physicists and ghostbusters and mediums and psychics and a whole slew of other so-called experts out here doing séances and what have you, all to figure out if it's really him."

"Do you think it's him?" I asked.

"I *know* it's him," Eugene said with total confidence. "I'm here at all sorts of hours when nobody else is around. I've seen that shadow. I know what you're talking about."

"Why do you think he's haunting the place?" I asked.

"Ain't that obvious?" Eugene asked. "He wants to know how he died. Classic ghost story, right?"

It sure was. A classic *unfinished* ghost story. That's why the book was in the Library. This was Baz's story. Theo and Lu's cousin were just bit players.

"And nobody knows exactly what happened?" I asked.

"If they did, Baz probably wouldn't be here anymore," Eugene said wistfully. "You know, rest in peace and all that."

I debated with myself about how much to tell this guy. But he seemed open to the idea that things weren't always what they seemed to be.

"Maybe I can help," I said.

Eugene sat down in the seat across from me and looked me square in the eye.

"Now, how would you do that?" he asked skeptically.

"Do you believe Baz could see into the future?" I asked.

Eugene gave it a couple of seconds' thought, then nodded. "Yes, I do."

"Then maybe you'll believe I can look into the past."

"How so?" he asked with interest. "You got your own crystal ball?"

"Sort of," I replied. "I know what happened the night Baz was killed."

Eugene's eyes went wide as if the news shocked him. "You do?"

"Yeah. There was a kid at Playland. Derby was his name. About nine years old. His parents ran a concession stand. He was afraid of the dark, and there were these kids teasing him about not wanting to go into the Magic Castle alone. So Derby went in, but he brought a candle with him, probably to see by. Big mistake. The candle lit some hanging ropes on fire."

Eugene's mouth dropped open in shock. His face had fallen as if he'd seen a ghost. Which he had, I guess. That much had been established.

"How could you know that?" he said, barely above a whisper.

"I told you—I can see into the past."

"But I've never heard anybody say anything about that," he said, numb. "You couldn't have read that in a book."

I laughed. I really did. If only he knew. But I wasn't going to get off track.

"It's not in a book," I said. "Not really. I saw it. Call me an oracle too. Or whatever you'd call somebody who sees things that already happened."

"So you think this kid Derby killed Baz?" Eugene said. "Sounds to me like it was an accident."

"I don't know if it was an accident or not, but I don't think the fire Derby started burned the Magic Castle."

Eugene sat bolt upright. "Why? I thought you said—?"

"Because I saw what really happened. Derby may have deliberately set a fire with that candle, or maybe it was an accident. I don't know. But there's no way a fire that big and spread that fast started with a little candle flame. It was a freaking inferno! The fire that killed Baz had to have started another way."

Eugene stared at me with wide eyes. He was the self-appointed historian of Playland but had no clue about how the most dramatic event in the park's history had played out.

But I did. Sort of.

"So then who set it?" Eugene asked eagerly.

"I don't know," I said. "But if I can figure that out, maybe Baz can rest in peace. Then maybe he'll lighten up and let me take a peek into that crystal ball."

"What for?" Eugene asked, confused.

"I don't think Baz had the power to see the future," I said. "Not on his own, anyway. I think it's all about the crystal ball. Baz only looked into it, like watching a TV. If I can take that crystal ball and get it near my friend, maybe I can see something that'll help us figure out what's going to happen to him tomorrow."

Eugene scratched at his chin thoughtfully. "Quite the story," he said. "Explain to me how exactly you've come to know all this again."

"I told you," I said. "I can look into the past. Call me

a reverse psychic. What I can't do is see the future. For that I need the crystal ball."

Eugene looked at the ground, deep in thought. I was asking him to help me commit a crime. If we got caught, he'd probably lose his job. Or end up in jail. Probably both.

"Tell me, chief," I said. "Do you think the future is set, or can it be changed?"

He looked up, still in thought. His eyes traveled across the vintage pictures of Playland that hung on the walls.

"I'd like to think we have a say in our own futures," he said thoughtfully. "What we can't change is the past. That we have to live with."

"Yeah," I said. "Nothing we can do about the past, except maybe learn the truth."

Eugene looked me straight in the eye. "You really think that kid didn't set the fire?" he asked.

"No, he started a fire all right. I just don't believe it was the fire that killed Baz."

"And you can prove it?"

"I can try," I said. "You say you love this park? Imagine if you could solve the big mystery that's been haunting the place for decades. I can do that. I can find the truth. But I'll need your help."

Eugene brightened. He liked that idea.

"Maybe I can run a little interference for you," he said. "No promises. Baz isn't the friendliest character."

"You get no argument from me," I said. "He was a jackwagon when he was alive too."

Eugene gave me a strange look.

Maybe I'd gone too far. I jumped to my feet and exclaimed, "Let's do it!" before he could change his mind or ask any more questions.

We hurried across the rapidly brightening park, headed for the arcade. With the warm sun finally hitting the buildings along the midway, color returned to Playland and the place looked a lot less eerie. I pushed all thoughts of a sword-swinging ghost out of my head. I was going to get the crystal ball and have a shot at saving Theo. My plan was to take it home, get it to Theo, look to see what danger he was headed for, and make sure he avoided it. Then after I returned the crystal ball, I'd go back into the book and figure out what really happened that night. That would finish the story. Baz's spirit would learn the truth and be able to move on. Classic. No more haunted amusement park. Eugene might even come out looking like a hero.

But first . . . Theo.

When we entered the arcade, I was on high alert, scanning for any sign of a shadowy sword-swinging demon trying to keep me from the machine. I didn't know what I'd do if he showed up. I had to hope Eugene would somehow keep him away from me.

"Make it quick," Eugene said with a shaky voice. He sounded as nervous as I was.

I took out my screwdriver and went back to work on the last few screws in the door of the fortune-telling machine.

"If Baz shows up, tell him we're trying to help him," I said.

"I don't know if that ghost listens to reason," Eugene said. "I've had a couple of run-ins with him."

"Tell me about it," I said. "He didn't listen much when he was alive either."

Eugene gave me a strange look. Again. But I ignored it. Again.

I added, "I guarantee he won't be happy about somebody messing with his crystal ball, so if you see anything—"

"Hey!" somebody shouted. "What the heck are you doing!"

We had company, and it wasn't a ghost.

I spun around to see two security guards hurrying our way.

What I *didn't* see was Eugene.

"It's okay!" I called to the guys. "I'm with Eugene."

I kept working on the screws, still thinking I could get the crystal ball out of there.

I was wrong.

"Put that down, kid," one of the guards commanded. "Now."

He was talking about the screwdriver. It was a weapon. The two guards stood behind me, keeping a safe distance in case I lashed out or something.

"Eugene!" I shouted. "Little help, please!"

No answer. Eugene had bailed.

"You got a friend here?" one guard asked.

"Yes! It's Eugene. The other security guy."

"Ain't nobody here named Eugene," the guard said. "Just drop the screwdriver, kid. We don't want this getting ugly."

My mind was racing. How could this guy not know Eugene? I doubted they had a very big security staff. I looked back at them and saw that the two guys were wearing khaki uniforms with dark green jackets. Eugene's uniform was navy blue. Why was that?

The truth hit me in the gut.

Eugene wasn't a real guard. He probably didn't even work at the park. He was just as much an intruder there as I was. He was probably some freak who liked hanging around the old park. I couldn't believe how he threw me under the bus like that.

I dropped the screwdriver and looked at the two guys, wondering if they'd believe the story about Baz's ghost and the crystal ball that told the future and my friend who was going to die the next day.

Their sour faces told me all I needed to know.

I was done.

They each grabbed one of my arms and hustled me out of the arcade.

"I wasn't breaking anything," I argued lamely.

"Didn't look that way to me," one guard said gruffly.

"We'll let the police decide," the other said.

My stomach dropped. I had gone from thinking that everything was falling perfectly into place to realizing that everything was falling down on my head. What was I going to tell my parents? I'd been in trouble before, but nothing like this. We're talking arrest-and-police-record-type trouble. In the meantime, Theo was still in danger.

This story was about to come to a close, and it wasn't going to be a happy ending for anybody.

The two guards brought me back to the kitchen where Eugene and I had talked about fixing everything. What a joke. We'd been there only ten minutes earlier, but it felt like a lifetime. My mug of hot chocolate was still on the table. It was still hot.

"Cops are on the way," one guard said. "Don't cause any more trouble."

"Don't worry," I said glumly.

He had no idea that I was actually trying to stop trouble from happening

"Hey," I said. "You're seriously telling me you don't know anybody named Eugene who hangs around here pretending to be a security guard?"

The guy thought for a second and said, "I've been working here over thirty years, kid. Last person named Eugene left around the time I started. But he was an old coot back then. Can't imagine he's still around." He laughed and added, "Unless he's a ghost, that is."

With that, he slammed the door and locked it.

His words made my head spin.

Playland was haunted, all right. But just *how* haunted?

My mind flew back to all the things Eugene had said about the park, about its history and about how much he cared about it. He knew all about Baz, too, and the fact that his ghost was haunting the midway. I glanced up at the wall and the old photos Eugene had been looking at. This kitchen held an entire history of the park. Besides old shots of the midway and the various rides, there were tons of group photos of staff through the years. Some pictures looked ancient and yellowed, as if they'd been there since the park opened. Others were more recent. One was taken only last year. It was set up like a team photo with all the employees sitting in the band shell, where concerts were held. I glanced at the photo and picked out the two security guards who had nabbed me.

There was no Eugene.

What was it the guard had said? *I've been working here over thirty years, kid. Last person named Eugene left around the time I started.*

When would that have been? The mid-1980s?

I walked along the wall, scanning the photos, looking for a staff picture from that time. I finally found one that was in color, but faded. It was another team photo taken in the band shell. A cute girl in front held a sign that said *1985.* My eyes moved quickly over the faces, one by one. All the girls had big hair, and many of the guys had mustaches. It was definitely from another era. I was starting to feel dumb, when my eyes landed on a guy on the far end of the back row. Was it Eugene? The image was pretty small, so it was hard to tell, but he was wearing the same kind of navy-blue uniform Eugene had on. It could have been him, but if it was, he didn't look any younger than the guy I'd been talking to.

Below the photo was a list of names, left to right, row by row. I did a quick scan to find the name of the guy in the last row.

When I found it, I felt as though my head was about

to explode. Was it possible? Was it a coincidence? Or was there more than one ghost hanging around Playland?

The name of the guy in the last row was Eugene, all right. But there was more.

His name was Eugene Derby.

Derby.

Was this the grown-up version of the kid I'd met in the book in 1937? It was possible, I figured. The math worked. He would have been around sixty in the 1980s. But the math fell apart when you tacked on another thirty or so years to bring him to today. Eugene wasn't ninety years old. If the Eugene Derby I'd met was the same Derby from the story, then there was only one possible explanation.

Playland was being haunted by two ghosts, and maybe this story wasn't just about the Oracle Baz.

A flashing red light painted the wall. The police had arrived. I was about to be arrested. It was a helpless, hopeless feeling. Once they got me, any chance I had of helping Theo would be gone. I was trapped in that room with no way out.

Wait.

I *always* had a way out. I could get out by going in . . . to the Library.

I quickly reached under my shirt, grabbed the

Paradox key, ran to the locked door, and held the large brass key out toward the doorknob. Instantly, the wooden surface beneath the knob went molten, and the round brass plate appeared that held the keyhole. Everett was right. The magic worked on any door. I inserted the key, twisted, and felt the familiar sensation of the heavy tumblers clicking into place.

My plan had changed. Before doing anything to help Theo, I had to do all I could to solve the mystery surrounding the death of the Oracle Baz.

I pulled open the door and let out a relieved breath.

I was back in the Library.

CHAPTER

13

On Saturday morning, Lu sat with her aunt and uncle in front of Jenny's computer screen, watching intently with tired eyes.

"This is futile," Uncle Nathan said, exasperated. "It's a shot in the dark. One in a million. We're wasting our time."

"Oh?" Aunt Tina said coldly. "Is there something more important you'd rather be doing?"

Uncle Nathan didn't respond to that. He sat there quietly, chastised.

The three had been up all night at the computer. Waiting. And waiting. And waiting some more. While they took turns trying to get some sleep in Jenny's bed, one person stayed focused on the screen.

Hoping. Praying.

The night before, soon after Lu had charged into her aunt and uncle's room to wake them, they had started a Skype account under Lu's name and a Facebook account for her aunt Tina. Both sent a friend request to Jo Wong. Since they had already discovered that Jenny's phone wasn't working, the hope was that Jo Wong's was. Or better still, that she would log on to Skype or Facebook and discover that Jenny's family was trying to reach her. Every fifteen minutes they made a Skype call to Jo's number, and every fifteen minutes it wasn't answered.

"I think we should call the police there," Uncle Nathan said. "They have a better chance of tracking her down than we do."

"But where would we call?" Lu asked. "Which police department?"

Uncle Nathan wanted to answer, but he stopped because he knew Lu was right. That would be another long shot.

"Let's give this a few more hours," Aunt Tina said. "If we don't hear anything, we'll have to take a stab and call our own police department, and maybe they can suggest–"

"Wait!" Lu exclaimed.

The screen changed. After hours of painful, anxious waiting, someone was answering their Skype call.

"Oh my God," Aunt Tina said with a gasp.

All three crowded around the monitor. Nobody was breathing. Seconds felt like days as they stared at the small screen that would reveal who was answering their call. Their plea. The smaller window was dark, then suddenly flipped to an image. It was distorted by slow computer speed, but it was unmistakable.

Jo Wong had answered the call. She looked out at them from the computer screen.

"Hello?" Jo said. "Annabella?"

Aunt Tina gasped.

"Yes!" Lu exclaimed in a loud, clear voice. "This is Annabella. Can ... you ... hear ... me?"

Jo laughed. "Sure. I'm in Australia, not on Mars. What's up?"

Jo's casual response took everyone by surprise.

"What's up?" Uncle Nathan exclaimed while crowding next to Lu. "Are you kidding me? Where is my daughter?"

"Mr. Feng?" Jo said. "Are you there too?"

"And so am I!" Aunt Tina said, pushing next to Lu.

Now all three could be seen huddled together in their own window.

"Where is Jenny?" Aunt Tina demanded.

Jo scowled. She didn't expect to answer the Skype call and be attacked by three very anxious people. She looked off camera and said, "I think they want to talk to you."

"Jenny!" Aunt Tina yelled. "Are you there?"

She strained to see who Jo was talking to, as if moving to the side would let her see around the corner, off-camera.

Jo slid out of the shot, and another girl took her place.

It was Jenny.

Alive and well.

"Hey," Jenny said with a smile. "Is there a problem?"

The three sat there with mouths open in shock. Nobody knew how to react. It was Uncle Nathan who was finally able to speak.

"You're okay?" he asked tentatively.

"Of course," Jenny said, laughing. "Why wouldn't I be?"

The three shared stunned looks. In that moment their emotions sped from nervousness, to relief, to confusion, and finally . . . to anger.

"Are you kidding me?" Lu shouted. "Problem? Yeah, there's a problem! You disappeared for weeks! Nobody knew what happened to you!"

"What?" Jenny said, shaking her head. "That's not true. I left a note."

"What note?" Uncle Nathan exclaimed. "I didn't see any note!"

"I put it on the kitchen counter the day before I left," Jenny said. "It explained everything."

"There was no note on the counter," Aunt Tina said.

Uncle Nathan ran out of the room, headed for the kitchen.

"Well, that's where I left it," Jenny said. "In an envelope with your names on it. It explained everything."

"Why didn't you just tell us you were going to Australia with your friend?" Aunt Tina asked, tears forming in her eyes.

"Because you would have told me not to go, Mom," Jenny said. "You know that. Jo had a great opportunity. A whole semester in Cairns to study erosion of the Great Barrier Reef. She asked me to tag along, and all I had to do was come up with the airfare. If I had told you I wanted to go, you would have gone off on how irresponsible it was and how I couldn't miss work, and you would have done everything you

167

could to stop me. So I didn't ask. I left you a note and took off."

Uncle Nathan came back into the room holding a note and the envelope it had been in.

"It was stuck in a pile of junk mail," he said. "We must have dumped the mail on the counter and scooped it all up together. Jenny, why didn't you just tell us you wanted to go?"

"Because you would have stopped me, Dad. You know that."

"Then why didn't we hear from you?" Aunt Tina asked.

"My phone doesn't work in Australia," Jenny answered. "And you guys don't go online. I left you numbers to reach me, but when you didn't call, I figured you were mad and didn't even want to talk. We Skype with friends from Internet cafés all the time. We just logged on, and when Jo saw that Annabella had an account, she answered right away."

Uncle Nathan examined the note. "All her numbers are right here," he said, dazed, still trying to get his head around what had happened.

"We're not mad at you, Jen," Aunt Tina said.

"I am, a little," Uncle Nathan said.

"We were so worried," Aunt Tina said. "We

didn't know where you were or if something terrible had happened."

"I'm sorry, Mom. I really am. I didn't mean for you to worry. But there was no way I was going to miss out on this chance. I mean, it was a once-in-a-lifetime opportunity."

Lu took the fortune card from the desk and read from it. "'Seize the moment. You may not get another opportunity. Follow your heart.'"

Jenny laughed. "You found that? That card is the reason I'm here. A dumb fortune I got from a machine at Playland. I actually followed the advice. If I hadn't gotten it, I wouldn't be sitting here right now. Can you believe it?"

"Yeah," Lu said. "I can."

C H A P T E R
14

I blasted into the Library, yanked the Paradox key out of the lock, and slammed the door shut behind me before I could be spotted by any cops or security guards. I made sure the door was shut tight, then spun around to come face to face with Everett, who was clutching the black book.

He looked pissed. His head was going bright red again.

"You are playin' with fire, boy-o!" he exclaimed as he shook the book at me angrily. "You can't go breakin' laws, no matter how important it may seem. You go and get yourself locked up in jail, you won't be doing anybody any good. Especially yourself."

"Yeah, that was a close one," I said as I hurried past him.

"It's *still* a close one," he exclaimed as he fell in behind me. "When you return, you'll be going back at the exact same moment you left. The police will still be coming for you."

Oh. Right. Forgot about that.

"Yeah, well, I'll figure something out," I said dismissively.

I went right to the circulation desk and reached below it to pull out the 1937 clothes I'd need to wear to blend in at olden-day Playland.

"You were right, Everett," I said. "There's way more to this story than we thought. It's not just about Baz. Two ghosts are haunting Playland. Baz and Derby. They're in limbo because neither of them knows what really happened the night Baz was killed. My guess is Derby thinks he's the one who killed Baz. He left a candle in the Magic Castle, and a fire burned the place down. That's his disruption. His spirit is probably trapped there as punishment. But it's not the end of the story. There's no way that little fire would have spread so quickly. I think the fire that killed Baz was set some other way. That's what I've got to figure out."

Everett flipped through the pages of the book quickly, scanning for details.

"I agree. The timing doesn't seem to add up," he said as his spectacles slid down onto his nose. He was gradually calming down and focusing on what needed to be done, rather than on the trouble I'd gotten myself into.

"As long as Baz's spirit is hanging around Playland, protecting that machine, there's no way I'll be able to nab that crystal ball," I said.

"I believe the police will have something to say about that as well," Everett added.

"But if I can find the truth about what really happened that night, it might free up Baz and Derby so they can move on and leave Playland. That'll give me a shot at getting the crystal ball and figuring out what's going to happen to Theo tomorrow."

"Simple as that?" Everett asked.

"Simple as that," I replied.

"I do hope you're right," he said. "Do you have a plan for sleuthing out the truth?"

I pulled the sweater over my head and jammed on the floppy hat.

"Move the bookmark," I said, gesturing to the black book. "Make it earlier that day, before the fire. I'll stake out the Magic Castle. As soon as somebody does anything suspicious, I'll have 'em."

Everett took out the red bookmark and flipped through some pages, looking for the exact right spot in the story for me to enter.

"You're a thinker, lad," Everett said, chuckling. "Just like your father."

I headed for the door on the far side of the Library, the one that would take me back into the story. Everett was right on my heels while flipping through the book.

"You need to be careful, Marcus," he said. "If somebody has enough evil in their heart to murder Baz, they won't think twice about hurting anyone who finds them out. The stories in the books may exist in their own dimension, but when you're in it, you can still get hurt."

"I'm not going to be a hero," I said. "I just want the truth."

"Which would make you a hero," Everett said.

That made me smile. "Yeah, I guess it would."

Everett closed the bookmark into the book and held it to his chest. "And that's how you'll finish the story," he said with confidence.

I reached for the door and said, "No, the story won't be finished until Theo is safe and we find Lu's cousin."

"Aye," Everett said. "Good luck to you, lad. Keep your wits about you."

"Always do," I said, and opened the door that took me back into the workshop next to the carousel . . . in 1937.

★   ★   ★

The park was alive with people and excitement. I had gotten used to jumping back and forth in time, so I didn't stop to gawk at the differences between Playland then and now. I just thought of it as two different places. When I stepped out of the carousel roundhouse, I saw that the sun was still up but shadows were growing long. If Everett had stuck the bookmark in the right spot, it was the afternoon of the big bad night. I had plenty of time before the fire would be set.

I wasn't exactly sure what I should do, so I headed for the Magic Castle, thinking I would scout for any service doors that a killer could use to get inside and set a fire. On my way I passed a crowd of people gathered beneath a huge ladder that stretched straight into the sky. It had to be over a hundred feet high. At its base was a small pool of water that wasn't much bigger than a backyard kiddie pool. On top of the ladder was a small platform, where a woman in a sparkly bright-red bathing suit stood. It made me dizzy just looking at her up there.

There was a drumroll coming from a guy standing near the base of the ladder. All eyes were on the woman. She was actually going to jump from that crazy-high perch into that little pool of water. If that wasn't nuts enough, a guy walked up to the pool with a flaming torch and touched it to the rim. Fire spread quickly, forming a burning circle.

My mouth went dry. It was insane . . . and awesome.

The drumroll stopped. There was a long moment of silence as everybody held their breath, including me.

The woman jumped. She plummeted, picking up speed quickly. She did one twist, one somersault, and *boom!* She hit the water with a thunderous blast. Water erupted from inside the pool, dousing the flames.

I still hadn't taken a breath. Was she okay? A couple of long seconds passed where I wasn't so sure, but the woman suddenly popped up from beneath the surface, thrusting her arms to the sky in triumph.

An announcer called out, "Let's hear it for the one, the only, Daring Donna!"

The place went nuts with applause. I clapped too. I wasn't sure if it was out of respect for an incredible stunt or with relief that she hadn't gone splat. A small band kicked in with an old-fashioned marching song as the woman climbed out of the pool and walked a victory lap around it while waving to the crowd. It wasn't until then that I recognized her. I think it was more the bathing suit I remembered than the woman herself. It was the lady who Baz and the worker-guy in coveralls had been fighting over.

Daring Donna. The name fit. She was daring, all right. I kind of wished they still put on nutty stunts like this at Playland, but times were different then, I guess. It made me want to stick around to see what other death-defying shows they had going on, but I was on a mission and time was moving.

Looking past the crowd, I saw the familiar spires of the medieval-looking attraction that was the Magic Castle. The last time I had seen that building it was being destroyed by fire. But that wouldn't happen until later that night. At the moment it was clean and intact. I couldn't help but smile. Moving that bookmark around really did change where I entered a story. Amazing.

I had gotten halfway across the midway when I was shocked to see Baz headed my way. He wasn't wearing his robes, but it was hard to miss him—he was so tall. His tight goatee was a dead giveaway too. The guy looked to be on a mission of his own. He strode quickly through the crowd with his head held high, as if he were operating on a more important level than the rest of us lowly peasants.

I followed him at a distance and had trouble keeping up with his long strides. People had to dodge out of his way or he would have walked right over them. I, on the other hand, had to snake in and out to avoid people.

Baz walked to the far end of the midway, opposite from where his show tent was set up. This was the Kiddie-Town section of Playland. He turned off the midway onto an intersecting sidewalk that led to a large wooden structure. It was a dome that covered an open-air dance floor. There were no shows going on, so the place was empty.

Almost empty. A woman sat alone on a bench outside the building.

It was Mrs. Simmons, the wife of the guy Baz had predicted would die. She still didn't look so hot. Her eyes were red and puffy as if she'd been crying. Her hands were folded in her lap, where she nervously twisted a handkerchief.

Baz strode right up and stood over her, his long shadow throwing her into darkness.

I crept close and found a spot behind a tree that was close enough for me to hear what was going on, but not close enough to be spotted.

Baz glared down at her.

Mrs. Simmons kept her eyes on her hands, as if afraid to look up at him.

What was Baz doing? This poor woman had been through enough. She didn't need any more grief from this ego-case.

"Dear Mrs. Simmons," Baz said in a voice that was surprisingly gentle. "Thank you for meeting me."

Mrs. Simmons lifted her chin, though she was too shy to make eye contact.

"What is it you want?" she asked in a meek voice.

"May I sit?" he asked politely.

She nodded, and Baz lowered himself onto the bench next to her. She sat there, stiff, as if the very presence of Baz was like sitting next to a disease.

"No words can tell you how sorry I am about the loss of your husband," Baz said with what sounded like genuine sympathy. "I have no control over the visions I see. Oftentimes I learn of joyous news. Other times I receive warnings of grave danger. I regret that I was unable to convince your husband of the peril that awaited him."

Huh? Baz actually sounded human.

Mrs. Simmons sniffed and said, "The things you see—are they images of a future that's meant to be? Or does it create the future?"

Baz gave the question some thought and said, "No one can create someone else's future. I certainly cannot. We all have choices. I simply see shadows of the way things might be."

"So you had nothing to do with the accident?" she asked.

"Goodness, no!" Baz said, appalled. "I have no control over people's lives."

Mrs. Simmons nodded thoughtfully and said, "So if he had listened to you and gone home, would he have been saved?"

"I believe so," Baz said. He looked to the ground. It

was his turn to have trouble with eye contact. "Forgive me for not being more forceful with my warning. It is a regret I will forever carry with me."

"That must be a burden," she said. "Being able to see things like that."

Baz shrugged, keeping his eyes down. Mrs. Simmons reached out and patted his hand. She was actually consoling him.

"It's all right," she said bravely. "Wasn't your doing. You tried to save him. Thank you for that."

Baz gave her a weak smile and reached into his jacket to take out an envelope.

"This is for you," he said. "It isn't a lot of money, but hopefully it will help you to make ends meet during this difficult time."

Wow! Could it be true? Was Baz actually a softy?

"I can't take your money," she said. "Times are tough for everyone."

"It isn't all from me," Baz said. "Every employee here at Playland contributed what they could. We're a family, and we've lost one of our own. Please, we all want you to have it."

Mrs. Simmons looked at the envelope, then took it and immediately burst into tears. She leaned into Baz's shoulder, and he offered her a consoling hug.

I couldn't believe what I was seeing. I thought Baz

was an arrogant jerk, and maybe he was. Or maybe that whole superior thing was part of his act. But the guy went out of his way to take up a collection to help out the poor lady. It made me think that having the power to tell people's futures might not be such a great skill. I wouldn't want that kind of pressure.

So Baz was actually human. Go figure. More important, he said the words I was desperate to hear. The future that crystal ball shows, the future he sees, doesn't have to come true. He used the magic word: *might*. I liked might. That meant things could be changed. There was hope for Theo. All we had to do was figure out what he had to be careful of.

Baz stood up, gave a respectful bow to Mrs. Simmons, and headed back the way he had come. I skirted the tree so he wouldn't see me and then followed him again. I was feeling bad for the guy. He was going to die that night. Knowing he wasn't a total jerk made his death seem that much more pointless. He might have had enemies, but he also had a heart. The Oracle Baz was a way more complicated guy than I had thought. More than ever, I wanted to solve the mystery of his death and free his spirit from the park. He deserved that.

He was almost back to the midway when a man leapt out from behind a concession stand. The guy grabbed

Baz by the shirt and pulled him behind the small structure. Baz was caught totally by surprise. The guy started
whaling on him, punching him in the stomach and ribs.
Baz didn't stand a chance. The guy threw four or five
solid punches that made sickening thuds when they hit.
He would have kept going if a woman hadn't run up and
pulled him away from Baz.

"Stop it, Ron! You'll kill him!" she shouted.

I recognized the guy. It was the boyfriend who had
threatened Baz with the sword. The woman was his
girlfriend. Daring Donna. Her hair was still wet from
her death-defying leap into the flaming pool.

The angry guy, Ron, pulled away from the woman
and leaned down to Baz, pointing a threatening finger
at him. "I'll kill you, all right," he snarled. "You won't
always have somebody around to protect you."

The guy straightened up and grabbed the woman's
arm, ready to storm off. But the woman yanked her arm
back. By then a crowd had gathered, and Ron didn't look
like he wanted to make a scene, so he left Daring Donna
standing there and hurried off.

Donna went right to Baz, who was trying to sit up
but was having trouble. He was hurting.

"I'm so sorry," she said. "Now you know why I don't
want to be with him anymore. His temper is horrible."

"My dear Donna," Baz said, clenching his teeth to fight off the pain. "He is a coward. He never would have gotten the best of me if I had seen him coming."

"That's just it," she said. "You'll never see him coming."

"Not true," Baz said with a small smile. "I see all sorts of things. Don't fear for me, my dear. Worry about yourself. Stay away from him. If you need my protection, you have it."

"Thank you, Baz, thank you," she said.

Daring Donna backed away and melted into the crowd that had circled Baz. Everyone stood there, staring in wonder.

Baz stood up straight, grimaced in pain from the effort, gave a theatrical bow, and announced, "And that, my friends, is the end of the matinee. Be sure to attend my show tonight for a far more interesting and enlightening performance."

He strode off with his head held high as people laughed and clapped.

Gotta admit, the guy had style.

I followed him as he made his way back toward his show tent. He wasn't walking as quickly as before and was hunched over a little. I think the beating Ron had given him had done some real damage. It explained why Baz was in so much pain during the performance he would give later that night. He probably had a couple of busted ribs.

Ron had suddenly become my number one suspect. He'd threatened to kill Baz, and Baz would be killed that night. It didn't take Sherlock Holmes to connect the dots. But I had to know for sure, which meant I probably had to catch Ron in the act of setting the fire.

Waiting for Baz outside his show tent was Hensley, the park manager.

"You're a fool, Baz," Hensley said.

Baz strode right past him to the tent. "I've been called worse," he said as he disappeared inside.

Hensley followed him, and I quickly snuck in after them. I crouched down near the door, where they couldn't see me but I could still hear what was going on.

Baz went straight up onto the stage and began polishing the various swords he used in his act. He wasn't moving as smoothly as before. He was definitely hurting from the beatdown he'd just gotten.

Hensley stayed on the floor in front of the stage, his hands on his hips, looking up at Baz.

"You're better than this," Hensley said. "You're doing a two-bit carny act for rubes when you could be rolling in it. You can see the future for Pete's sake! You can predict things that'll happen! Think of how much that could be worth! Tell me who's going to win the World Series—I'll bankroll the bets. We'll clean up. Look into that ball of yours and see who's gonna be the next heavyweight champ and we'll be rich. You tell me things that're gonna happen, and I'll find a way to turn it into cash. What's stopping you?"

Baz stayed focused on the sword he was polishing. "My gift is a responsibility, not an asset," he said. "I have ethics."

"Ethics schmethics!" Hensley exclaimed. "Where do you think your paycheck comes from? It's from the saps who pony up good coin to come to this park and watch you show off that so-called gift. I don't see you turning down that money. Ethics go out the window when it comes to cold hard cash."

"Indeed," Baz said. "Anyone who would skim a percentage from Playland's daily receipts has no ethics whatsoever."

Hensley stood up straight as if Baz's words had hit him like a bolt of lightning. "What're you sayin'?" Hensley asked.

"There is much about the future that I see," Baz said. "It's quite the disturbing burden to learn someone close to you has done something horrid. It raises the question, what should I do with that knowledge? I'm sure the police would love to hear my tale."

"Are you threatening me?" Hensley said, his anger growing.

He made a move to step up onto the stage, but Baz quickly pointed his sword at the man. Hensley stopped short.

"I'm telling you that I know what you've been doing," Baz said. "You're a thief, Hensley. You're stealing from every last person who works at this park when you skim the gate receipts. And you wouldn't even contribute a dime to help Simmons's widow."

"It was an accident! Accidents happen! Wasn't my fault."

Baz straightened up as if Hensley's words had a horrible odor. "You will resign from Playland," Baz said coldly. "Now. Today. Do that and no one will ever learn of your odious little thefts. You have my word. Take your money and go. But if you stay, I don't need to look into your future to know it will involve a jail cell."

Hensley balled his hands into fists. If Baz hadn't been pointing a sword at him, I think he would have jumped up onto the stage and start swinging. There was a tense moment where the two stared each other down.

"Turn me in and you'll regret it, pal," Hensley said. "You can count on that."

"What I count on is never seeing you again," Baz said. "Now if you'll excuse me, I must prepare for my performance."

Hensley headed for the exit. "Watch your back, pal," he warned as he spun on his heel and hurried out of the tent.

I had to duck behind a large stand-up sign for *The Oracle Baz* so he wouldn't see me.

Baz went back to polishing his sword as if nothing had happened. The guy was icy cool, considering that his life had just been threatened by two different people. I now had two prime suspects who could have set the fire. Or who were about to set the fire. Somehow I had to figure out which one would do it, or if it was somebody else entirely. The only thing I felt certain of was that Derby hadn't done it. There was only one way to know for sure: I had to see it happen for myself. So I snuck out of the tent and headed for the Magic Castle.

Night had fallen. The lights of the park had sprung to life. I passed several people who were walking in the other direction, headed toward Baz's tent to get in line for the next show. After having been through it all once already, I figured I had about twenty minutes before Baz would see something disturbing in his crystal ball and suddenly end the performance and go back to the Magic Castle.

Sometime between now and then, the fire would be set.

I had to be there when it happened.

CHAPTER
15

The sawhorse with the *Ride Closed* sign stood sentry in front of the Magic Castle, just as it did the last time we had visited the story. I guess I could say history was repeating itself, but it was more like I was living in the memory of what had happened years before. Books from the Library were gateways into other dimensions where these unfinished stories floated around, unbound by time, repeating themselves until the disruptions were ended. What had actually happened, happened only once. It couldn't be changed. Not in real life, anyway. The best we could do was snoop around inside these stories like archaeologists trying to uncover hidden truths that were lost in time.

But I wasn't a spirit. I could get hurt. If anything happened to me, it would be very real. The last thing I wanted was to become a spirit myself and have my story told in a book shelved in the Library. That would suck.

I walked over the footbridge, straight for the ride. In a few minutes this entire structure would go up in flames. I'm no expert, but something like that doesn't happen quickly. The fire from Derby's candle couldn't have spread that fast. So unless there was a huge explosion that nobody knew about, the fire would have been burning for a while before people realized what was going on. For all I knew, it was already burning. That thought got me a little panicky, so I picked up the pace.

I walked past the main entrance and rounded the building, looking for another way in. I pushed aside bushes that grew around the base of the structure, looking for a service entrance that might be hidden from public view. I was moving away from the lights of the park to an area where nobody went unless they worked there. I wished I had thought to do this before the sun went down; it was getting hard to see.

I came around to the back side of the building and spotted a small light hanging from the wall, halfway along the length of the ride. Yes! There was only one reason to have a light back there. I jogged across the grass with my eyes focused on it. When I passed through a line of bushes that came out perpendicular to the building, I saw what I was looking for:

The light marked a doorway with the words *Staff Only* stenciled on it. I held my breath and grabbed the knob to find . . . it was unlocked. I was in! Just inside the door was a flight of stairs leading down to what was probably the basement. Not that I'm a pyromaniac or anything, but if I were going to light a building on fire, I'd probably start it in the basement, so that's where I needed to be. I hesitated a second and took a whiff, afraid I might smell smoke. I got nothing. My eyes weren't burning either. I felt pretty confident that the fire hadn't started yet. I wasn't too late.

As I grabbed the handrail and started down, I got a sick feeling in my stomach. What was I doing? In a few minutes this entire building would be swallowed in flames, and I was headed for the basement. This was crazy! I told myself I'd take a quick look to see if there was anything suspicious and then get the heck out of there.

Though my legs were shaky, I continued moving down. The whole way I kept telling myself that I'd be out of there in a few minutes.

The only light came from one bare bulb that dangled from above the stairs. Its glow was bright enough that

I could keep moving without falling and breaking my neck, but not enough to see much else. It created more shadow than light. When I hit the bottom, there was only one way to go. A narrow corridor stretched into darkness directly in front of me. I had come this far—I had to keep going.

Slowly, cautiously, I moved ahead. Creeping around in the dark didn't feel much different from walking through the twisting corridors of the attraction itself. I was once again moving along a narrow, dark corridor. Only this time Frankenstein and Dracula wouldn't be popping out at me. At least I hoped not. I made it to an open doorway and leaned inside. In the dim light I made out what looked like an electrical panel. This was where the power came into the building. If an electrical problem started the fire, this was probably where it would begin. But nothing looked out of the ordinary. (Not that I knew what was normal for an electrical room in 1937. Or in my time, for that matter.) I left the room and moved on.

I was beginning to think this was a waste of time and I had totally misguessed how and where the fire would start. Time was ticking and I hadn't learned a thing. I was pushing my luck, so I turned to retrace my steps and get out of there, when I sensed something.

I didn't see it or hear it.

I smelled it.

Gas, I said to myself.

My nose was hit with the distinct smell of some kind of gasoline. Or maybe it was kerosene. Or paint thinner. Or turpentine. I didn't know exactly what it was, but I'd helped my father paint enough times to recognize the sharp smell that came from the liquid we used to clean brushes. Smelling too much of that stuff killed brain cells.

And, oh yeah . . . it was totally flammable.

Was gas spilled somewhere? Had some bumbling painter left cans open? Or knocked them over? That was the exact kind of thing that would lead to a fire. If there was enough flammable liquid around, it could burn big enough to start a fire that would spread quickly. All it needed was something to ignite it.

My brain screamed, *Run!* However the fire was going to start, it would happen soon. If I was anywhere near the fuel, I wouldn't stand a chance.

But I couldn't leave. Not when I was so close to learning the truth and ending this story.

I forced myself to keep walking ahead to follow the scent. With each passing second I felt as though I was that much closer to solving the mystery, while also moving closer to my doom. A few yards farther on I came to a closed door. Light leaked out from beneath it. Had the fire already started in there? Or was it just a light on the other side? I told myself that finding the answer to that question would be my last act before getting the hell out of there.

As I crept closer to the door, the strong smell grew more intense. Even with the door closed I could smell it. I had the brilliant idea to put my hand against the door to feel if it was hot. If a fire was raging on the other side, I'd feel it. But the door was cool. I touched the metal doorknob. That would definitely be hot if the room was on fire. It wasn't. It gave me the confidence that I still had time to get out . . . but not until I found out what was on the other side.

Clang!

Something had fallen down on the other side of the door. It sounded like a metal can had hit the cement floor and bounced a few times. Was somebody in there?

I had to know so I grabbed the doorknob, twisted it, and pushed the door open.

The large room beyond was dimly lit by a couple of overhead bulbs that let me see deep inside. The room was vast, but with a low ceiling. And I was right: the smell was some kind of paint thinner. The strong smell hit me hard as soon as I stepped through the door. This was where all the paint for the park was stored. There were hundreds of cans and larger metal tubs stacked everywhere. Most had been used and had paint drippings all over them.

The smell of turpentine, or whatever, was so strong it burned my nose. How could that be? I didn't think that one can of stuff left open would create such an intense smell. I took a few steps into the room and scanned the space. I didn't see any sign of a fallen tub or can. But it sure smelled horrible. My eyes were watering. I walked in farther. If this is where the fire was going to start—and it sure looked like it was—there had to be something to ignite it. Fires didn't just start. What was that called? Spontaneous combustion? We'd talked about that in science class. Unless there was high pressure or heat or some other factor, the only thing that would ignite a fire was a flame. Or a spark. But there was nothing around that looked like it could do that.

At least that's what I thought.

I was so incredibly wrong.

I saw a flare of light that came from beyond a wall of stacked paint cans. If I'd been smart, I would have turned and run out of there, but I guess I wasn't that smart. I was drawn to see what it was. I moved quickly to the wall of cans, stepped up on a stool, and peered over the top.

The paint cans were stacked to form a barrier that separated one section of the room from the next. On the other side I saw a person dressed from head to toe in black. Even his head was covered with a hood. The room was so dark and the shadows so deep that I couldn't see who it was. But whoever it was, he was up to no good.

The floor was wet, and not with water. That answered the question of why the gas smell was so strong. The entire floor was covered with the flammable liquid, and it was obvious how it had gotten that way. In one hand the person in black held a metal can that he was using to shake more liquid over a stack of paint cans. In his other hand he held a stick that had one end wrapped with cloth to make a torch . . . and it was burning.

Everything I had guessed was true. Derby's candle hadn't burned down the building. It was arson. And given what happened to Baz, it was murder. But proving all my theories correct didn't feel much like victory just then. I was about to witness the torching of the Magic Castle, and I was standing square in the middle of it.

"Don't!" I screamed out.

The person in the hood shot a surprised look my way . . . and tossed the torch. The stick spun across the room, landed in a puddle of flammable liquid, and ignited it. Flames spread quickly across the floor and crept up the many cans of paint that were stacked everywhere.

I still didn't know who the pyro was, and I no longer

cared. I had to get out of there. I was about to jump off the stool when the hooded figure suddenly ran toward me and flung himself at the wall of paint cans. The wall toppled on me, knocking me off my feet and sending me crashing to the floor as heavy gallon cans of paint thudded down, bouncing around me and pounding every inch of my body. I wrapped my arms around my head for fear a heavy can would hit it and knock me out cold. I took a couple of hits on my arms, but I was too amped up to feel any pain.

Once the avalanche ended, I looked around to get my bearings. I had to get out of there, but which way? Flames were now crawling up the walls. The heat was making me dizzy. It wouldn't be long before the entire room was a furnace. I spotted the door I had come in through and scrambled to my feet. But before I could take a step, an eruption of fire created a wall of flames between me and the escape route. The fire must have hit a barrel of kerosene—because it went off like a bomb. The wave of heat nearly knocked me onto my butt. It pushed me back but didn't burn me. At least not yet. I was trapped by a wall of fire that stood between me and safety.

I stood there in brain lock, not knowing which way to turn. The heat was getting so intense that breathing it into my lungs made me cough. The toxic smell probably had something to do with that too. I was in serious trouble.

But so was the pyro. Where was he? Did he get out?

I caught a fleeting glimpse of the dark figure on the far side of the room, deep in the depths of the basement, running for his life. But to where? He sprinted to a set of rickety wooden stairs that led up to a door. A door. Escape. Safety. It probably led into the castle itself. It didn't matter, as long as it got me out of there.

I'd gotten what I came for. Sort of. I didn't know who set the fire, but I found out for sure it wasn't Derby. That would have to be good enough. Maybe this was Derby's story after all. Maybe his spirit was doomed to haunt Playland because he mistakenly thought he had set the fire that killed Baz. I'd tell him the truth. It wasn't him. He'd be set free. I still wanted to know who set the fire, but I also didn't want to be barbecued.

It was time to get out of there and go home.

As I ran for safety, I pulled the Paradox key from around my neck. It didn't matter to me where the door at the top of the stairs led to. It was going to get me back to the Library.

The fire was spreading quickly. It was right on my butt and closing fast. The whole building was about to go up in flames. I choked on fumes and coughed so hard my head spun, but I kept going. When I reached the bottom of the stairway, I climbed two steps at a time. The flames had already hit the rickety wooden stairs and were traveling up fast, engulfing them. Fire licked through the open stairs, curling over them, destroying them faster than seemed possible.

I stayed focused on my target. The door. It wasn't a normal door. It didn't have a doorknob or a standard doorframe. It looked like it was just a section of wall with hinges. I had a moment of panic, thinking the Paradox key might not work because this wasn't a proper door. At the top of the stairs was a small platform. I stopped there and reached forward with the key.

The keyhole appeared, right where it always did.

"I am so out of here," I said.

But I wasn't.

Before I could stick the key into the keyhole, the door swung open and the pyro lunged out at me. He grabbed me by my sweater, swung me around, and pinned me against the wall next to the door. This guy was powerful. I didn't stand a chance.

"I can't let you go," the guy said in a raspy, desperate whisper.

I reached up and grabbed the hood that covered the guy's face. I had to know who he was. Hensley? The jealous boyfriend? Or was it somebody else who wanted Baz dead?

I yanked the hood off and came face to face with the pyro.

The truth made my head spin.

He wasn't a he.

It was the lady who Baz and the jealous boyfriend were fighting over.

Daring Donna turned out to be a whole lot more daring than anybody imagined.

"Why?" was all my brain could think to get my mouth to say.

The woman's eyes were wild with crazy, and she actually smiled.

"Because I love him," she said almost sweetly.

Crack!

The rickety wooden stairs were about to collapse. The whole structure jolted as if ready to pull away from the wall and send the two of us crashing down into the inferno. The woman fought to keep her balance while still clutching my sweater. She was strong too. Athlete strong. She pivoted and pulled me away from the wall, trying to fling me off the stairs.

I reached back at the last second, grabbed the side of the door opening, and held on for my life. No way I was letting go.

Donna couldn't pull me loose and she knew it. She let out a guttural, almost inhuman cry of frustration and let me go while leaping through the door to safety.

I spun around while still clutching the doorframe for fear she would try to push me back from inside. But she was gone. I guess she was more worried about saving herself than finishing me off.

Crack!

The stairs collapsed. The platform fell away beneath me, crumbling into a well of fire. I held tight. No way I was losing my grip and taking a death fall. I managed to swing my leg up and catch the other side of the opening. From there I hoisted myself up to safety.

Safety? I was still only a few feet above a raging inferno that was gathering strength. A quick look around showed me that I was in a dark, narrow corridor. It was a little cooler away from the fire, but that wouldn't last long. I had only a few seconds to take a deep breath and to try and figure a way out of there before the fire burned up through the floor. My best chance of escape was still plan A. The Library. The door was still a door. It would get me out of there. All I had to do was open it with the Paradox key.

The Paradox key.

The key I no longer had.

I felt as though my brain exploded. The key had been

in my hand when Daring Donna attacked me. It wasn't anymore. At some point I had dropped it while I was struggling with her. Where the hell was it?

I crawled to the doorway and looked out onto the basement room that was no longer a room. It was hell. Fire had engulfed the entire space, fueled by paint and all sorts of other flammable liquids. I looked directly down to where the stairs had been to see nothing but flames. The heat was so unbearable it took my breath away. In that one horrible second, I was hit with a sickening realization.

I wasn't just stuck in a fiery nightmare; I was trapped in this story.

CHAPTER
16

I couldn't leave there without the Paradox key. If I did, I'd never leave there at all. I'd be stuck in the other-worldly limbo of this story for . . . what? The rest of my life? Would my parents even know I was gone? Would time at home stand still until I found another way out? How long would that take? Was it even possible?

What if it took years and I showed up at home as an old man? At least then I wouldn't have to worry about the cops—they wouldn't be looking for an old codger. But my parents would never see their son again, because I'd be older than them!

Fire or no fire, I had to find that key. Spending the rest of my days in somebody else's story was not an option.

All those thoughts took about four seconds to race

through my head. If the key had fallen into the fiery basement below, I was done. I had to hope that I'd dropped it somewhere near me . . . and that I'd find it before the flames burned the floor beneath me.

I pulled myself back in through the doorway and looked around to see nothing but dead black. Even the light from the fire didn't help me see anything, because my pupils must have contracted. I got on my knees and swept my hands back and forth across the floor. It was the only way I had of searching.

But now the floor was getting hot as the flames built up below. I feared that at any second I'd hear a crack, the floor would give way, and I'd tumble into the fiery furnace. But I kept searching. To give up would mean my life was over. But staying there much longer *really* meant my life would be over.

Flames suddenly licked up through the floorboards in front of my face. The surprise knocked me back onto my butt. Time had run out. It was now about survival. I had to get out of there. I struggled to my feet as the corridor suddenly lit up with a bright light. I thought for sure the fire had engulfed the space and I was a goner, but instead of the sound of crackling flames, I heard a loud school bell.

I'd heard that sound before. What was it?

Looking up, I saw the Frankenstein monster leering

at me from behind a chicken-wire fence. I was in the Magic Castle ride. The light came from the dumb exhibit. Something must have triggered it.

"You looking for this?" somebody said.

I saw the silhouette of a person standing in the corridor in front of me. The guy had something in his hand that he was holding out to me. It dangled from the end of a cord. My brain flashed back to Michael Swenor's ghost and the times he had offered me the Paradox key. But this wasn't Michael Swenor. Or a ghost.

It was Derby.

"What're you doing here?" he asked, breathless. He sounded as panicked as I was.

I could have kissed the kid. Instead, I jumped to my feet and snatched the key out of his hand.

"Trying to get out," I yelled. "Where do we go?"

"That way," he shouted over the roar of the flames, pointing behind me.

Crack!

The floor gave way beneath Derby. He screamed in terror as his foot broke through.

I lunged forward, grabbed him, and pulled him toward me. No way I was gonna let anything happen to him, even if he was a spirit from another time.

"Move!" I shouted, and the two of us stumbled back along the dark corridor, headed for the ride's exit. Or entrance. I didn't care which, as long as it got us out of the fire.

"This is the way I came in," Derby said with authority.

He grabbed me by the wrist and led me forward, making quick twists and turns through the labyrinth. The light from the fire behind us made it way easier to navigate than when Lu and I had been there before. The air grew cooler as we got closer to the entrance. I could breathe again. After a few more turns, I heard the music of the park. We were leaving the real terror behind and returning to the land of make-believe thrills.

The escape route brought us to the entrance of the ride. We burst out from the doorway into the cool of the night to see fire trucks headed our way, their red lights blazing as they rolled cautiously across the midway to avoid curious onlookers.

"Keep moving," I commanded. "The whole building's going up."

To get clear of the doomed castle, we ran across the drawbridge that spanned the moat. I looked back and saw the turrets already enveloped in flames. Baz had once again died a fiery death.

When we were far enough away to feel safe, we stopped to catch our breath.

Two cop cars were parked on the edge of the

midway, keeping people back and clearing a path for the firefighters to get through.

When I finally focused on Derby, I saw that he was in tears, and not just from the smoke.

"It was an accident, I swear," he said frantically. "I didn't mean to start the fire. I was just . . . scared."

"You didn't start it," I said.

"Yeah, I did!" Derby shouted. "I brought a candle in there. It was stupid, but those guys wouldn't cut me any slack. I thought if I went through once, they'd leave me alone. But they followed me in and jumped me and . . . I dropped it. I gotta turn myself in."

Derby started for the cops, but I stopped him.

"You didn't start it, Derby," I said. "No way the fire from a candle would spread this fast."

"But the ropes were on fire," he cried. "I couldn't put it out. I got scared and ran. That's when I heard something that sounded like a fight. I beat it through the ride, and when Frankenstein lit up, I saw you. And that key."

"You saved my life," I said as I slipped the Paradox key back around my neck. "If not for you, I'd still be in there."

And stuck in this story forever. And dead.

"Yeah, but if not for me, there wouldn't be no fire," he argued.

"I'm telling you—I know who started the fire, and it wasn't you."

"Donna!" somebody yelled.

Running past us, headed for the police, was Hensley.

We followed him as he hurried toward two policemen who stood on either side of a woman. Baz's girlfriend. Or Ron's girlfriend. Or both. Daring Donna. The pyro. Her face was covered with soot and ash. When she spotted Hensley, she threw her arms around him.

Uh . . . what?

"Isn't that the lady Baz and that guy were fighting over?" Derby asked. "Why's she hugging Hensley?"

Good question. Really good question.

"Are you okay?" Hensley asked Donna.

"You know this lady?" one cop asked Hensley.

"Yeah, she's my girlfriend," Hensley replied, then focused on Donna. "Why are you all dirty? Were you in there?"

"Yeah, she was," I called out. "She's the one who started the fire."

Everyone shot me a surprised look.

Hensley was absolutely stunned. He kept throwing confused looks between Donna and me.

That was it. That's when it happened. It was the moment the story changed, because the mystery had been solved.

The disruption was over.

"Who are you?" Hensley finally asked, taking an angry step toward me.

One of the cops held him back.

"I'm the guy who nearly got killed because your girlfriend set a fire in the basement," I said. "Ask her."

"What's he talking about?" Hensley asked Donna.

"It's okay," Donna said. "You're safe now."

"What did you do?" Hensley said with growing urgency.

"Baz can't hurt you anymore," she said while kissing the guy on the cheek. "Now you don't have to go away."

Hensley gazed up at the nightmare of the Magic Castle that was now completely engulfed in flames. The look on his face was one of pure horror as the truth became clear.

"That's why you asked me to close the ride?" he asked, incredulous.

"I didn't want anybody else to get hurt," she said. "I didn't know that kid would be in there."

"Surprise," I said.

"You did this for me?" Hensley asked, bewildered, like he couldn't wrap his head around it.

"Baz was going to have you arrested," she said innocently, as if it was the most obvious thing in the world.

"I didn't want that, and I didn't want you to leave. Now it's all okay."

Hensley pulled away from her as if she were toxic.

"This . . . this ain't right," he said, bewildered.

"You can say that again," one of the cops said as he pulled Donna away.

Daring Donna.

Demented Donna was more like it.

"I love you!" she called back to Hensley as they disappeared into the crowd.

Hensley looked dazed. He turned back to the Magic Castle just as the giant turret collapsed, sending up a huge spray of sparks.

"That's what she told me in there," I said to Derby. "She said she did it because she loved him. How seriously insane is that?"

"Donna sure has a lot of boyfriends," Derby said.

I took him by the arm and led him away from the scene as firefighters rushed forward with hoses to put out the fire that had already destroyed the building. It was too late for the Magic Castle, and for Baz. It was now about containing the fire and saving the rest of the cursed amusement park.

Derby and I got away from the crowd that had gathered to witness the horrifying spectacle. I had already seen too much fire to care.

"So it really wasn't my fault?" Derby asked.

"No, it was crazy Donna," I said. "You're off the hook."

Derby looked totally relieved. Then he glanced back at the fire, and his shoulders dropped. "This park ain't never gonna be the same," he said.

"Yeah, but you won't have to feel guilty about it the rest of your life," I said.

"Thanks, Marcus," Derby said with genuine gratitude.

"No problem," I replied. "Now I gotta tell your future self."

"Uh, what?" Derby asked, totally confused.

"Can I ask you a favor?" I said, changing the subject.

"Name it," Derby said.

"Come with me," I said, and led him away from the midway.

I took him to the building that held the kitchen where, decades from now, the security guards would stick me, waiting for the cops to arrive. I was relieved to see it looked pretty much the same as it did in my time, without all the photographs, of course.

The room was empty. Everybody was out watching the demise of the Magic Castle.

"You say you know everything about this park," I said. "If you were trapped in this room and people were coming for you, what would you do?"

"What do you mean?" he asked.

"I mean, is there a way to do the whole *Escape the Room* thing that I'm missing?"

"What's an *Escape the Room* thing?" he asked.

"It's an app that hasn't been invented yet."

"A what?"

"Doesn't matter. Is there another way to get out of this room if the door is locked?"

"Well, yeah," Derby said matter-of-factly.

"Show me."

He walked farther into the room and said, "This is the same building as the Ye Olde Gold Mine." He went behind a counter that acted as a serving bar, reached to the floor, and pulled open a trapdoor. "This goes right into the ride," he said.

For the second time that day, I could have kissed that kid.

"Yes!" I exclaimed. "You just saved my life again."

"I did?" Derby said, confused.

"Look, chief," I said, "I gotta go. Do me a favor and don't go starting any more fires, okay?"

"Hey, I learned my lesson."

"Great. See you in about eighty years."

Derby gave me a confused look and said, "You're kind of an odd duck."

"Yes, yes, I am," I said.

I left Derby in the kitchen and ran back to the maintenance room in the carousel house, where I dropped my sweater and hat in the lost-and-found bin. I wouldn't be coming back to this story again. It was done. At least this part of it, anyway.

I pulled the Paradox key from around my neck, wiped away some gray ash, and kissed it. Yes, I really kissed it. I held it out toward the closet door to see the keyhole appear. It was the most welcome sight I could imagine. I opened the door, and seconds later I was back in the Library.

"Ya gotta stop putting yourself in so much danger!" Everett exclaimed, waving the book at me. "It makes for good reading, but you're tempting fate, boy-o."

"It's not like I had a whole lot of choice," I said as I walked quickly through the Library, headed for the door back home.

"So it was this Donna woman," Everett said as he followed me.

"Yeah, what a piece of work," I said. "She had three different boyfriends fighting over her and killed one to protect another. Yikes."

"Didn't see that one coming," Everett said. "My money was on Hensley being the culprit. You did a fine job, Marcus. The story's ended."

"Not yet it isn't," I said. "We ended the disruption, but Theo's still in trouble and Lu's cousin is still missing."

"But she isn't!" Everett exclaimed. "They found Jenny!"

I stopped short, and Everett nearly ran into me from behind.

"Really?" I said.

"She went on a trip and left a note that nobody saw. The fortune told her to seize the opportunity, so she did. She's in Australia."

"She's okay?" I asked.

"Fine and dandy."

"Excellent. Now all we've got to do is figure out how to protect Theo."

"Aye. But first you have to deal with the police coming to arrest you," Everett said. "You certainly seem to attract a lot of attention."

"Hey, it's not me!" I exclaimed. "Blame these stories you've got in here."

I stopped at the door that would lead me back to Playland. The present-day Playland.

"Do you have a plan?" he asked.

"You know something?" I said. "For a change, I do."

I threw open the door and stepped into my next crisis.

CHAPTER
17

As soon as I entered the kitchen, I ran straight for the far end of the room and the trapdoor that would be my escape route. The serving bar was still there, just as it was in the story.

"Where is he?" I heard somebody call from outside.

"Locked up in the kitchen," came the reply.

The silhouettes of two people moved by the window, headed for the door that would lead them to me. I was seconds away from handcuffs. No problem. I was also seconds away from getting out of there. But when I got behind the counter, I didn't see the trapdoor. My pulse shot through the roof. Had it been covered over? Had they put in a new floor? I forced myself to calm down and took a closer look. I realized there was a rubber mat covering it. I lifted it to reveal the metal ring in the floor that Derby had used to open the trapdoor. Yes! I quickly rolled the mat up and stuffed it under the counter.

The sound of footsteps outside grew louder.

I reached down, flipped up the ring, pulled, and . . . the door wouldn't budge. No! This thing probably hadn't been opened in years. Or worse, it might have been nailed shut. What was I thinking? What an idiot! The only thing I could do was use brute force to try and yank it open. I braced myself with both knees flat on the floor and pulled.

The trapdoor didn't move. But I didn't give up. What else could I do? I kept pulling for all I had until I thought I'd burst a blood vessel in my head. There was a brief crack and a slight movement. That only made me work harder. I released the pressure, then yanked again. Little by little, the hinge loosened until there was a sharp *crack!* The door pulled open with a loud creaking of rusted hinges.

There was no time to celebrate. I heard the jangle of keys outside the locked door. I yanked open the trapdoor and saw wooden steps leading down into the dark. I didn't know where they would take me and I didn't care, as long as they got me out of there. I slipped through the opening and pulled the door down quickly, hoping that nobody could hear the metallic squeal from the ancient hinges.

I sat there in the dark with the closed trapdoor inches above my head, not moving for fear that any sound would give me away.

The sound of multiple footsteps on the floor above signaled that the cops had arrived.

"Where is he?" somebody said, the voice muffled by the floor between us.

"We left him right here!" somebody else exclaimed. It was probably one of the park security guards. "He couldn't have gotten out. The door was locked!"

Somebody walked around, probably searching the room. I held my breath, fearing that any slight sound might give me away. If they walked behind the counter and looked down, they'd see the trapdoor for sure. I waited, expecting to hear the sound of footsteps directly over my head.

"Yeah, well, nobody's here now," somebody said.

"That's impossible!" somebody else exclaimed.

"Well, unless he was a ghost, I'd say it's possible," came the annoyed reply.

I almost laughed at that. Almost.

"Look, we've got better things to do than deal with kids running around your park," one of the cops said, sounding pretty ticked off. "You might want to try installing a better gate at the entrance."

"Tell me about it," the security guard said, defeated. "I've been telling them that for years."

"Do us a favor and kick the kids out yourself," a cop said.

"Yeah, whatever," the guard said softly.

The next sound I heard was a flurry of footsteps walking away and the kitchen door closing.

Thank you, Derby.

I didn't think it would be wise to open the trapdoor and leave through the kitchen, so I cautiously moved down the stairs to find another way out. Derby said the stairs led into the ride called Ye Olde Gold Mine. I'd done this ride a few times when I was a little kid. It was a boat ride through dark caverns made to look like a mine where little fairy-tale-like dwarfs worked to excavate gold. It had been around since the park first opened and probably hadn't changed much. I remember it being pretty scary when I was six.

At the bottom of the stairs was a door. It was the only way to go, so I pulled it open and stepped through . . .

. . . to find myself in a cavernous, make-believe mine. I could tell it was a mine because there were little dwarfs everywhere and according to fairy tales, mining was a popular dwarf profession. I guess they were supposed to look like Snow White's pals, with pointed caps and shoes, but there were a whole lot more than seven of them.

A few feet in front of me was the waterway the boats traveled on. The only light came from a single bulb that was probably a work light. The rocky cavern wasn't lit up the way it would have been when the ride was working. I remembered being afraid of the scene when I was little, and, to be honest, it still creeped me out. It was all too dark, and I kept expecting the dwarf dudes to come to life.

"I'm sorry," somebody said.

I think I jumped about a foot out of pure surprise. If a dwarf had come to life, I would have lost it completely. But when I spun around, I was relieved to see Eugene. Or Eugene's ghost. Weird to think that seeing a ghost could be a relief, but welcome to my reality.

"Jeez, you scared me," I said, trying to catch my breath.

Eugene stood at the edge of the waterway with his hands in his pockets.

"I didn't help you with the guards or the police," he said. "I guess you know that I don't really work here. At least not anymore."

"Yeah," I said. "That. And you're a ghost . . . Derby."

Eugene's mouth fell open with surprise. Kind of

strange to think that I had the ability to surprise a ghost, but that's the way my life had been going lately.

"But . . . how . . . I don't understand," Eugene said, totally stunned.

"I told you I can see into the past," I said. "And I've seen a lot. I know your parents worked a concession here when the park opened. I know you brought a candle into the Magic Castle and accidentally started a fire. And I know you think it was your fault the ride burned and Baz died."

Eugene stared at me in total shock.

"How is that possible?" he muttered.

"I'm standing here talking to a ghost, and you're asking *me* how that's possible?"

"If you saw what happened that night, you know why I'm still here. And why Baz is still here."

"I do," I said.

"I can leave, you know. Anytime I want. But I don't. I lived a long life. Baz didn't. It's my fault that his spirit is stuck here after suffering such a stupid, violent death. I won't abandon him."

"Yeah, well, that may be why you're here, but that's not why Baz is here," I said.

"What do you mean?" he asked.

"Can we go to him?" I asked.

Eugene nodded.

"But I don't want to run into those security dudes again," I said.

"You won't," Eugene replied. "It's their lunch break. They never miss it. I see it every day."

Eugene led me out of the creepy tunnels of the fairy-tale mine, headed back toward the arcade. The whole way there I kept looking over my shoulder, fearing that one of the guards would be out hunting for me. When we got back to the arcade, I walked right up to the Baz fortune-telling machine and looked at the dummy, whose gaze was fixed on the crystal ball.

"I know what happened," I said to the dummy. "I saw it all. I saw how you gave Mrs. Simmons money to help her out after her husband was killed. I saw how you got jumped by that jealous boyfriend who beat the snot out of you. I saw how you threatened to turn Hensley in for stealing money from Playland. I saw it all."

Eugene let out a sigh. "How could you possibly know all this?" he asked,

"Trust me," I said. "It's possible."

I turned back to the Baz dummy and said, "What did you see in the crystal ball the night of the fire? Why did you go back to the Magic Castle?"

The Baz dummy said nothing.

"They found his body in the ruins of his apartment," Eugene said. "He was clutching a suitcase. It was badly burned, but they could clearly see it was packed for a trip. People figured he saw the future, predicted the fire, and tried to get out with some belongings. But it all happened much sooner than he expected, and he got caught."

"Yeah," I said. "Makes sense. But you know what else I saw? Eugene Derby went into the Magic Castle with a lit candle. He dropped it and accidentally started a fire. But it wasn't the fire that burned the Magic Castle. I saw how the real fire was set."

I think Eugene was holding his breath, if ghosts had breath to hold.

"It was Donna," I said.

"Donna?" Eugene said. "Daring Donna?"

"She was daring, all right, and very busy. Seems like everybody was fighting over her. Baz got beat up because of her. And she had another boyfriend besides Ron. Hensley."

"The park manager?" Eugene blurted out.

"She knew that Baz was going to turn him in for stealing from the park, so she lit the fire to stop him. She did it to protect Hensley. I know. I saw it. She started the fire in the basement of the Magic Castle in a room full of paint and turpentine. That's what lit the place up. That's what killed Baz. You weren't to blame, Derby."

I looked to the Baz dummy, waiting for some kind of reaction, but got none.

"Are . . . are you sure?" Eugene asked tentatively.

"Positive," I said. "Baz's spirit has been trapped in this park because he didn't know the truth about what happened that night. Now he knows. Now he can leave. That means you can leave, too, Eugene. Derby."

Eugene looked uncertain, as if he wanted to believe me but was having trouble getting his head around something that for years he had felt certain happened in a completely different way.

"I didn't kill Baz," he finally said, as if trying the words on for size.

"If anybody's ghost should be stuck in this park, it's Daring Donna's. Though I wouldn't want to be here if she ever showed up. That lady's a wack job."

Eugene smiled, then chuckled as his eyes lit up with joy. "After all this time," he said, almost giddy. "I've lived with guilt my entire life, and beyond. I don't know what to say to thank you."

"You don't have to say anything," I said. "It's Baz I want to hear from."

I turned around to face the dummy.

The dummy had no reaction.

"Well?" I said. "Mystery solved, chief. You owe me."

The light winked on inside Baz's glass box. It made me jump because I really didn't expect to get a reaction. Surprise. The mannequin came to life, moving very machinelike as his arm swept over the crystal ball. I took a step back, not sure what to expect. At least the creepy little clown marionette next door wasn't moving again. That would have put me over the edge.

Baz lowered his hand to the box full of cards, lifted one out, and dropped it into the hole. It fell through and popped out of the slot in front.

I could only stare at it. I didn't want my fortune told.

"You gonna read it?" Eugene asked.

"Do I have to?" I asked.

"I would."

"Yeah, well, you're already dead," I said.

But I went for it anyway. I grabbed the card, took a deep breath, and flipped it over.

There was a single word on the card:

FREE

I could breathe again.

"Not yet you're not," I said to the dummy. "I bailed you out. You and Eugene. I want something in return. You told my friend Theo's fortune."

I held up the card with Theo's fortune on it.

LIFE AS YOU KNOW IT WILL END ON YOUR FOURTEENTH BIRTHDAY. HUMILITY.

"His birthday is tomorrow," I said. "I know the fortunes you tell can be changed. It's why you tried to get Simmons to leave the park before his accident, and I guess it's why you packed your bag to try and get away before the fire. Nobody's future is set. Everybody has control. I want to know what's going to happen to my friend."

The dummy stared blankly at the crystal ball. Nothing happened.

I turned around to look at Eugene.

The guy shrugged and said, "Maybe he doesn't know."

I spun back to the machine, ready to yank open the door and grab the crystal ball. "Talk to me," I shouted. "Or I'll break this glass and steal your crystal ball and find out for myself."

A blue light glowed from within the crystal ball. I was so surprised that I think I actually let out a gasp. The Baz dummy didn't move, but it didn't matter.

The crystal ball was alive.

I took a step closer and gazed inside. What I saw was like a frantic movie playing out in close-ups that flew by so fast it was hard to make out exactly what was happening. It was the same jumble of images I had seen before, only this time they kept playing. Over and over. It gave me more of a chance to register what they were and what they might mean. There was a flash of red, like sheet metal. There were fleeting images of people. One was a black guy I only saw from behind. Theo. He wore a bright blue shirt. A rubber tire spun by. Water sprayed. And then it all jumbled together in a way that told me there was going to be a horrific crash. The red sheet metal crumpled. The guy with orange hair flashed by. It was all so fast and frantic that none of it made sense. The same images played over a few times, like a movie on constant replay. But it was so jumbled that it was hard to tell exactly what it was showing me. Water, tires, blue shirt, orange hair, crumpled red metal, crash. After it repeated a few more times, the crystal ball went dark. The show was over.

"No!" I yelled with frustration. "I don't know what any of that means. It looked like a crash, but where was it? When? How is it going to happen?"

The dummy sat there like, well, a dummy.

I spun to Eugene. "Get him to come back!" I shouted.

But Eugene was gone.

I turned back to Baz.

The machine was dead. The lights had gone out. The crystal ball was dark.

The whole place seemed strangely still, and I was

feeling very alone. Playland had been haunted. I sensed it from the minute I showed up. It was alive with the dead.

Not anymore.

It's hard to describe exactly how I knew, but the park suddenly felt empty. Whether the curse that had plagued it from day one was broken or not, I couldn't tell. But I knew in my gut that the spirits were gone. Probably forever. The disruption was truly over.

Baz had told his last fortune.

And I still wasn't sure how to protect Theo the next day.

His birthday.

CHAPTER
18

"Australia?" I said, incredulous. "She went all the way to the other side of the world and didn't tell anybody?"

"She *did* tell," Lu replied. "She left a letter. But it got lost in a bunch of junk mail and nobody saw it."

We were hanging out in Theo's driveway so Lu could spin around on her roller skates. It was Saturday night. The night before Theo's fourteenth birthday. The day when life as he knew it would end.

"Why didn't she just talk to them?" Theo asked.

"You gotta know Jenny," Lu said. "She does things her own way. Drives my aunt and uncle crazy. She was sure they'd have been all negative about it and done everything they could to stop her from going. They're pretty conservative. So she did what her fortune told her to do, and now she's on the adventure of a lifetime."

I looked at the card from Baz's fortune-telling machine that held Jenny's fortune.

SEIZE THE MOMENT. YOU MAY NOT GET ANOTHER OPPORTUNITY. FOLLOW YOUR HEART.

"She followed her heart," I said.

"And yet another fortune came true," Theo added, sounding glum. "Good for her. Not so good for me."

"It came true because she made it come true," Lu said. "She didn't have to go on that trip. It was her choice."

"Fine," Theo said impatiently. "I choose not to die tomorrow. How do I go about making that happen?"

None of us had the answer.

"The fortunes don't have to come true," I said. "Baz tried to warn that Simmons guy, and he himself tried to duck out before the fire."

"Yet both he and Simmons died anyway," Theo shot back.

"But he warned that guy Ron about the truck that might hit him," I said. "And it didn't."

"Baz didn't say the truck was going to hit him," Theo argued. "He just said to look out for it. Totally different."

"Run it down again," Lu said. "What exactly did you see in that crystal ball?"

"It was a jumble of quick images, like shots of a movie," I said. "I saw people running around and tires spinning and something red crashed. There was a brief flash of Theo wearing a bright blue shirt, and a guy with orange hair."

"You've got a bright blue shirt," Lu said to Theo.

"Yeah, a couple. But I don't know anybody with orange hair. That's something, right?"

"And there was a ton of water too," I added. "Like spraying around."

"So does this mean I'll be okay as long as I don't wear a blue shirt?" Theo asked.

Again, nobody had an answer.

I stood up and brushed off my pants. "Lu and I will come over first thing in the morning," I said. "We'll stay with you all day. Nothing's going to happen to you."

Theo nodded, but he didn't seem all that comforted.

"I want to believe we have control over our future," he said. "But everything I've seen so far tells me we don't."

"But we do, and tomorrow we'll prove it," Lu said with conviction. "And finish this story once and for all."

———————————

THEO MCLEAN DIDN'T SLEEP well the night before his birthday. He kept staring at the clock next to his bed as the luminous numbers crept ever closer to midnight. Once the clock showed 12:00, it would signal the arrival of the day he had been dreading ever since he received the ominous fortune.

He watched with tired eyes as 11:59 turned to 12:00.

The moment he had dreaded for weeks had arrived.

For twenty-four long hours, he would be in danger.

He lay awake, staring at the ceiling as his mind raced ahead to places and possibilities. What could happen? What was lying in wait? Would it be obvious? Or totally unforeseen? Most important, what should he do to avoid the danger?

There was no way to know, and it kept him from getting much rest.

At 6:00 a.m. sharp, his bedroom door burst open, making Theo sit up in surprise.

"We're late!" his older brother Joe exclaimed. "Get your tail out of bed!"

Theo rubbed his eyes. Apparently, he had dozed off and was awoken by Joe's unexpected whirlwind arrival.

"Late for what?" Theo asked, groggy.

"Your birthday present," Joe replied as he tossed Theo a pair of khakis that had been neatly draped over a chair. "Oh yeah, happy birthday."

Theo caught the pants and started getting dressed, moving slowly. He was still half-asleep and not thinking straight.

"How can we be late for a birthday present?" he asked.

"It's a surprise from Mom and Dad," Joe replied. He reached into Theo's closet and pulled out a button-down shirt for his brother. A bright blue button-down shirt.

"I don't like surprises," Theo grumbled.

"Too bad," Joe shot back. "This was set up a long time ago, and we're not gonna miss it."

He tossed the shirt to Theo, who dutifully began putting it on. It wasn't until he'd gotten one arm in that he realized what he was doing and yanked the shirt off. "I'm not wearing that," he said with finality. He was officially wide awake.

"Wear whatever you want," Joe said. "Just hurry. Mom and Dad went to church and want me to take you. I am totally cool with that because it's gonna be great."

"Tell me what it is," Theo demanded.

"Not a chance," Joe said adamantly. "I was sworn to secrecy. They want it to be a surprise. But I overslept and now we're late. So move!"

Joe left the room, and Theo sat staring at the bright blue shirt that lay crumpled on the floor, where it would stay. He jumped out of bed and found a deep green turtleneck that he quickly pulled over his head. He slipped on his pair of well-polished Top-Siders without bothering to put on socks first and ran out of the room.

"Joe!" he called while hurrying down the stairs.

Joe came out of the kitchen, slurping from a bowl of cereal.

"I really don't want to go," Theo said. "I . . . I don't like surprises."

Joe gave him a scoffing laugh and said, "You'll like this one. Trust me."

"Tell me what it is."

"I can't. Dad would kill me. And he'll really kill me if we don't get there in time, so let's move!"

"Stop saying *kill*," Theo said.

Joe plunked the bowl down on a table, yanked

open a closet door, and pulled out a bright blue wind-breaker. He started to put it on as . . .

"No!" Theo yelled, and pulled the jacket away from him.

"Dude, what is your problem?" Joe shouted angrily.

"Don't wear that jacket," Theo commanded.

Joe gave him a curious look, then reached for another jacket.

"It's your birthday, so I'll cut you some slack," he said, pointing a finger at his brother. "But whether you like it or not, we're going. This is too good, and I get to go, too, so pull it together, all right?"

Joe grabbed a set of car keys off the table and went for the front door.

"You're gonna thank me for getting your butt in gear," he said. He gave his little brother a playful shove and left the house.

Theo was in a panic. He ran back upstairs, found his cell phone, and entered Marcus's number.

There was no answer.

"Turn on your phone, Marcus!" Theo yelled into his cell.

He punched out of the call and dialed Lu.

Joe laid on the car horn impatiently, making Theo jump.

Lu didn't answer either.

"Why aren't your phones on!" Theo exclaimed.

Joe hit the horn again. Theo was breathing hard. His heart raced. The walls seemed to be closing in on him. He ran downstairs, grabbed a sweater from the closet, and sped out of the house.

"What's the holdup?" Joe asked impatiently as Theo got into the car. "You ought to be excited."

"Trust me, I'm plenty excited," Theo said soberly.

Joe pulled out of their driveway and the two drove off.

"I don't think we should do this," Theo said nervously.

"You don't even know what it is," Joe replied.

"I know. But did you ever have an overwhelming feeling like something was going to happen? Something bad? It's not like you can explain it, but you feel it in the very core of your being. You know the path you're on is the wrong one, and the best thing you can do is cut your losses and just stay home."

Theo looked to Joe hopefully. Had he gotten through to his brother?

"No," Joe answered flatly.

Theo sighed and dialed Marcus again.

"Whoa!" Joe exclaimed, and hit the brakes.

"What!" Theo shouted in fear while gripping the seat.

The car skidded a few feet and screeched to a stop.

"That yellow light turned really fast," Joe said. "I nearly rolled through a red. Getting a ticket is the last thing I need."

"Maybe not the last thing," Theo said.

"What's that supposed to mean?"

"Nothing. I really don't want to do this, Joe. I'm not feeling so good. Can we please go home?"

"No!" Joe exclaimed. "Stop being such a wuss. Just relax and go with it for once in your life, okay?"

Theo sank back into the seat but kept his eyes on the road. He was ready to scream if anything even remotely dangerous crossed their path. Mostly he was looking for any red car that might be lying in wait, ready to speed out from a side street and crush them. His only consolation was that neither he nor Joe was wearing a bright blue shirt.

But that didn't mean somebody wearing a bright blue shirt wouldn't be driving a red car that was closing in on them.

Driving with Joe was the absolute last place on earth Theo wanted to be. He kept trying to call Lu and Marcus to let them know what was going on, even though there wasn't anything they could do to help him. Whatever was going to happen was going to happen. Theo was on his own, and to make matters worse, his brother was right there with him. Joe could be in danger too.

"Remember that fortune you got from that machine at Playland?" Theo asked tentatively. "The one that said you were going to be bitten by a dog, and then you were?"

Joe laughed. "Yeah, that was wack."

"Yeah, well, I got a fortune, too, and it said life as I knew it would end on my fourteenth birthday. Remember?"

Joe thought for a second, then looked at Theo and said, "That's why you're being all twitchy? You think that stupid fortune's gonna come true?"

"Well … yeah."

"It was a machine, idiot!" Joe exclaimed. "Those things can't really see the future!"

"What about Harry?" Theo asked. "His fortune said he was going to get some money, and he did!"

"Coincidence!" Joe said in frustration. "Jeez, you're like some kind of science nerd. Why are you suddenly believing in hocus-pocus?"

Theo crossed his arms and pouted. "You'd be surprised at how much I believe in."

"Well, keep it to yourself," Joe said. "Unless you want to get locked up or something."

They drove on in silence with Theo's eyes laser-locked on the road ahead.

A strong fall wind had kicked up, making the trees sway ominously. Theo glanced to the sky, expecting to see dark storm clouds. That might explain all the water Marcus had seen in the crystal ball. But the sky was clear and blue. Still, the tree branches swayed back and forth dramatically, as if waving a greeting to them. Or a good-bye.

The trip took them along local roads to the northernmost border of Stony Brook. It was a wealthy part of town with large homes, each surrounded by acres of wooded property. On Sunday morning there was little traffic, which suited Theo just fine. He finally started to relax, but that didn't last long.

Joe put on the car's directional signal to make a turn, and Theo finally understood where they were going.

"The airport?" Theo asked, incredulous.

"Almost there," Joe replied.

Theo wanted to cry.

The Stony Brook airport was a small field that was used mostly for private planes and a few commuter flights. If you didn't know it was there, you'd miss it. The final drive was along a half-mile road that was lined on either side by dense forest. The trees were bunched together so thickly that the strong wind barely touched them. It wasn't until the car got to the end of the road and broke out from the trees onto the airport property that the wind hit them again.

Theo's heart raced.

"This is the surprise?" he asked nervously. "We're going up in a plane?"

"No," Joe said.

Theo relaxed. There was no way he was going to fly in a plane.

"We're going up in a helicopter," Joe said. "Surprise! Mom and Dad got you a sight-seeing tour of Stony Brook and New York City. And I get to go along for the ride. Happy birthday!"

Theo grabbed the armrest of the car, trying his best not to puke.

CHAPTER
19

It was a jumbled-up movie that kept playing over and over in my head. As I lay in bed that night, I kept thinking about the images I had seen in Baz's crystal ball.

A crumpling section of red sheet metal.

Tires bouncing on pavement.

Water spraying.

Theo in a bright blue shirt.

People running and screaming.

A guy with orange hair.

It all played out in soft-focus bits and pieces. What was actually happening was impossible to understand, except that it didn't look good. It was chaotic and violent and made no sense. It made me appreciate Baz's true gift. He might not have been able to conjure images from the future; that was the job of the crystal ball. But he had the ability to interpret them. It made me wish I hadn't solved the mystery of what had happened to him back in 1937 and released his spirit from Playland. It would have been nice if he'd stuck around a little longer to help figure out what Theo was in for.

I finally drifted off to sleep. As much as my mind kept racing, my body was exhausted. It had been a wild adventure, and I was drained. I needed the rest because the next day might prove to be every bit as intense as the one in the story of the Oracle Baz. I had to be totally on my game.

Unfortunately, my game didn't start well.

I overslept. I'd wanted to get up really early and head right over to Theo's before he started his day. His birthday. But I slept right through my alarm. When I finally cracked open an eye, it was already six-thirty. Normally, that would be about four hours too early for me to get up on a Sunday, but not on that day. When I saw the time, I was hit with a shot of adrenaline that was better than any alarm clock. Suddenly, I was wide awake.

I instantly grabbed my cell phone to call Theo. But the phone was dead.

"No!" I said with frustration.

How could I have been so stupid as to not have plugged it in the night before? I really must have been beat. I snagged the charging cord and plugged it into the phone and had to wait for what felt like a lifetime for the power to kick in. Once it did, I went right to the phone app . . . and my stomach dropped.

There were five missed calls from Theo.

"No, no, no!" I bellowed.

Why do people always shout "no" when they see something they don't like? It's not like it'll change anything. Mostly you see that in movies, but I guess it happens in real life, too, because I definitely shouted "no" a couple of times.

And it didn't change anything. I had still missed five calls.

I immediately hit CALL BACK, but it went directly to his voice mail.

"No!" I shouted with frustration.

The shouting didn't help that time either.

My next call was to Lu, and it also went to voice mail.

I didn't shout "no" again. I guess I finally realized how futile it was. I kept my head and called the McLeans' house number.

Again, I got voice mail.

It was six-thirty on a Sunday morning. Why wasn't anybody home? The McLeans belonged to a church on the other side of town, and they often went to the earliest, crack-of-dawn Sunday service. Theo hated that.

There was a good chance they were there. That realization made me feel a little better. Nothing can happen to you when you're at church, right? Right??

My last-ditch effort was to call Lu's home phone. It rang and rang, and just when I was about to scream "no!" into the phone like a fool, somebody answered.

"Hello?" said somebody who sounded half-asleep. I guess they weren't used to getting phone calls this early on a Sunday morning.

"Hi, sorry to call so early," I said. "Is Annabella there?"

"Marcus?" Lu replied.

"Yes!" (I don't mind saying "yes" when things go well. That's perfectly acceptable.) "Theo's been trying to call me, but my cell was dead," I said quickly because there was no time for formalities. "Did he call you?"

"I don't know," she said groggily. "Let me check."

She dropped the phone, and I waited for what felt like an hour before she got back. She was suddenly as wide awake and alert as I was.

"He's been calling me too," she declared. "But I turn my phone off at night. House rules. Why is he up so early?"

"Don't bother trying to call back," I said. "His cell goes to voice mail and nobody answers at his house. I'm thinking they all went to church."

"What do we do, Marcus?" she asked nervously.

Up until that moment Lu had been rock-solid confident that we could control Theo's fortune. Hearing the uncertain tension in her voice made me feel like at this point even she had doubts. We had planned to be with Theo the entire day, and we had already blown it.

"Let's go to his house," I said. "If they went to church, they'll be back soon."

"And what if they're someplace else?" she asked.

"Then I don't know," I said.

"Get out of the car, Theo," Joe demanded.

"I'm not going," Theo replied stubbornly.

"This cost Mom and Dad a truckload of cash. You can't chicken out."

"Oh, but I can."

"I don't get it," Joe said with frustration. "You always say you want to fly in a helicopter. This is your dream come true."

"Or my nightmare," Theo shot back.

"I'm not gonna fight with you," Joe said, trying to contain his anger. "But I'm not gonna take the blame for this. Let's go inside and talk to the pilot. If he can't convince you to go, then we'll call it off."

Theo thought about that and opened the car door.

"I don't care what the guy says," Theo declared.

"There's nothing he can say that'll make me fly today."

"Whatever," Joe said. "At least I can say I did all I could to make you not be a weezer. Let the pilot take the heat."

Joe was obviously disappointed because if Theo wouldn't go, he wouldn't get to go either.

They were parked in front of a small building that was marked with a sign: *Nimbus Air.* It was on the far end of the airport, a good distance from the main terminal building. Beyond the squat one-room building was a wire fence that cordoned off the runways.

Theo got out of the car . . .

. . . and left his cell phone on the front seat.

"I've got an idea," Theo said with enthusiasm. "I'll fly, but not today. Let's see if he'll change it to next week."

"Next week isn't your birthday," Joe said.

"Who cares?" Theo shot back. "I'm not six years old. It doesn't have to be on the day."

"What's the difference if it's today or next week or next year?" Joe asked.

"Next week I won't have this same bad feeling," Theo replied.

"Unbelievable," Joe said with exasperation. "It was a stupid fortune-telling machine, fool."

Theo could only shrug.

The two walked across the gravel parking lot toward the small building. Theo looked out beyond the wire fence to the tarmac. What he saw erased any last doubt that he was making the right decision. Sitting on the tarmac, not far from the building, was a helicopter with the name *Nimbus Air* painted on it.

The helicopter ... was bright red.

His stomach twisted and his head went light. The prophecy was becoming clear. It was foreseen that he would die in a tragic helicopter crash.

But not if he had anything to say about it.

I sped on my bike to Theo's house even though he lived only a few blocks away through the suburban sprawl of our neighborhood. I got there in record time, dropped my bike while still moving, and rang the doorbell, hoping Theo would throw open the door and tear me a new one for not answering his calls.

He didn't. Nobody did. Nobody was home.

"Are they here?" Lu asked as she flew in on her bike behind me.

"Only if they're asleep," I said. "But I doubt it."

"We let him down, Marcus," Lu said, near panic. "I promised him we wouldn't let anything happen."

"It's okay. They're probably headed back here right now."

"And what if something happens on the way? We should have slept here. Or had him stay at your house. Or tied him to a chair. Anything! We totally dropped the ball."

"I know, but it's still early," I said calmly, though I was feeling anything but. "His birthday is all day. He'll be home soon."

"Let's hope so," Lu said.

"You must be the McLean boys!"

Theo and Joe were greeted inside the small office by a tall, trim sixtyish African American guy wearing a leather flight jacket. His short gray hair and neat clothes pegged him as the pilot.

"I'm Captain Russell," the guy said warmly, holding out his hand to shake Joe's.

"I'm Joe. This is Theo."

"The birthday boy!" Russell exclaimed, and shook Theo's hand enthusiastically. "Fourteen. Great age. Old enough to get around on your own and start figuring out how it all works. Happy day."

Theo shook his hand and noticed that Russell was wearing a bright blue shirt underneath his leather jacket. The sight actually gave him confidence. This might have been the guy Marcus saw in the crystal ball. Things were playing out exactly the way the fortune had predicted. The only thing missing was somebody with orange hair.

Theo relaxed. This was where he was destined to meet his fate. He was sure of it, and he knew exactly what he had to do.

Or not do.

"Thanks," Theo said. "There's a change in plans, though."

"Oh?" Russell said, looking concerned. "Everything okay?"

"Here we go," Joe said, rolling his eyes.

———

Lu and I sat down on the front steps of the McLean house, leaning into each other to keep warm. A biting-cold wind whipped across the yard. It was the kind of morning best spent in bed, nice and warm. Asleep. And safe.

"Look!" Lu exclaimed.

A car turned off the road into the driveway.

"Yes!" I exclaimed.

Again, that's allowed.

We jumped up and ran to the car to find it wasn't Theo or his parents. Sitting behind the wheel was Harry McLean, one of Theo's older brothers. The one who went to college.

"No," Lu said with disappointment. And of course it changed nothing.

Harry opened the door and climbed out.

"Good to see you guys too," Harry said sarcastically. "What're you doing here so early?"

"Looking for Theo," Lu said. "Nobody's home."

"They're probably at church," Harry said as he got out of the car. "My parents love that early-bird service. Crazy. Still feels like last night to me."

"I thought you were at school," I said.

"I want to surprise Theo for his birthday," Harry said. "And have Mom do some laundry." He reached into his backseat and pulled out a sack stuffed with dirty clothes.

"We tried to call his cell, but he's not answering," Lu said. "We don't know your parents' numbers."

"We'll call 'em from inside," Harry said. "But I don't want to bother 'em during the service."

"They won't mind," I said quickly.

Harry gave me a *how would you know that?* scowl and headed for the house.

"I WANT TO POSTPONE the flight," Theo said adamantly.

"Really?" Russell asked. "Why's that?"

"Because he had his fortune told and it said he was going to die on his birthday," Joe said with a scoff. "Can you believe it?"

"Really? What kind of crazy fortune is that?" Russell asked, incredulous.

"*Crazy* is the exact right word," Joe said.

"It's dumb, I know," Theo said. "Nothing's going to happen. But I really don't want to tempt fate. Call me superstitious, or dumb, or whatever you want, but I'm not going to fly today. Maybe we can do it next week."

Russell gave Theo a curious look, as if not sure how to respond to such a silly concern. "The deal your parents made was for today," he said. "Rescheduling wasn't an option."

"So then let's fly!" Joe exclaimed.

Theo's shoulders fell. He was out of options.

But Russell gave him a big smile and clapped him on the shoulder. "I'm just giving you a hard time," he said with a laugh. "You actually saved me the trouble of delivering the bad news."

"What bad news?" Theo asked.

"We can't fly today," Russell said. "The winds are

crazy. Besides being dangerous, it wouldn't be a very pleasant experience. We'd be bouncing around like popcorn. Maybe that fortune of yours isn't so foolish after all."

Joe's mouth fell open. "Whoa," he muttered.

"Really?" Theo asked with total relief. "We can reschedule?"

"Absolutely," Russell said. "Have your parents call me, and we'll pick another day that won't be so dramatic." He smiled broadly and added, "For any reason."

Theo grabbed Russell's hand and shook it furiously. "Thank you, sir, thank you," he said, bubbling over with excitement. "I really want to do this. I do. I've always wanted to fly in a helicopter. Did my parents tell you that? It's been one of my dreams. It'll be awesome. Just not today."

Russell laughed. "Yes, it'll be awesome. We'll pick a perfect day."

Theo backed out of the room. "We will. Can't wait. So ... see ya!"

Joe looked to Russell and gave him a shrug.

"He's odd," Joe said.

"That's okay. Odd is good."

Joe went outside and looked to the car, but Theo wasn't there. He glanced around and saw his brother standing at the wire fence, staring out at the red helicopter.

"So everybody's happy," Joe said. "Let's go home."

Theo didn't move. He continued to stare at the helicopter, his excitement suddenly gone.

"What's the matter now?" Joe asked.

"Nothing. It's just kind of scary," Theo said. "I've been worried about this for so long. I feel like I just dodged a bullet. That's pretty intense."

"You are seriously strange," Joe said. "Tell you what: I'll get you home, and you can hide under your bed for the rest of the day. Maybe that'll make you feel better."

"Nah," Theo said. "I'm actually feeling okay."

Harry dumped his bag of dirty laundry on the stairs and went straight for the kitchen.

"You guys want something to eat?" he asked.

"Yes," I said.

"No," Lu said at the same time.

"Let's call your parents first," I said.

"What's the rush?" Harry asked.

"We just want to know if they'll be back soon with Theo," Lu replied. "You know, so we can figure out if we should hang out and wait or not."

"Whatever," Harry said, and pulled out his cell

phone. "I'll FaceTime them. It'll freak them out to see I'm calling from the kitchen. I didn't tell 'em I was coming."

Harry found their number in his contact list and hit the FaceTime button. The phone rang a few times, and then . . .

"Hey!" came Mr. McLean's voice through the phone. "What're you doing up so early on a Sunday? No party last night?"

"Yeah, there was, and I'm not feeling so hot right now," Harry said as he held the phone up so the camera would see him. "You see where I am?"

"You're in the kitchen!" Mrs. McLean exclaimed. "What're you doing home?"

"I came for Theo's birthday."

"That is so sweet!" Mrs. McLean said.

"And to do laundry," Harry added.

"And that is so typical," Mr. McLean said.

"Put Theo on," Harry said. "He's got a whole birthday committee here waiting for him."

Harry directed the phone toward Lu and me so we could see Mr. and Mrs. McLean and they could see us.

"Morning!" I said brightly. "Could you put Theo on so—"

The words caught in my throat.

"Oh no," Lu whispered in dismay.

"He's not here," Mrs. McLean said. "He's with Joe. Wait'll you hear what his birthday present is."

I didn't register anything they were saying. All I could do was stare at Mr. McLean.

The guy was wearing a bright blue shirt.

Life as Theo knew it was going to end that day, but not because of anything that might happen to him.

The person in real danger was his father.

CHAPTER
20

At just past dawn, a small group of teens stood around in the empty parking lot of Stony Brook Middle School, stomping their feet on the leaf-strewn blacktop to try and stay warm. They clutched cups of Starbucks coffee for warmth, yawned, and generally fought to keep their eyes open at an hour that was so crazy-early the sun was barely peeking over the treetops.

"Why are we doing this so early?" a kid with a hoodie pulled tight over his head asked nobody in particular. "On a Sunday. It's crazy."

A tall guy with blond hair cut so short he looked bald was the only one who didn't seem annoyed to be there or bothered by the cold. He leaned against a jet-black Mustang like he owned it, with his arms casually folded across his chest.

"No problem, you can sleep in next time," he said to his friend with no sympathy. "We'll visit you in the hospital."

"You know why we're doing this now," another guy said impatiently. "We've got the whole block to ourselves."

A girl with a bold streak of purple in her long dark hair glanced at her cell phone.

"We're in the window," she said. "Church got out ten minutes ago. If we don't go soon, traffic's gonna start picking up again."

"He's not coming," the kid with the hoodie said, annoyed. "I knew he wasn't coming. I got out of bed for nothing. I'm gonna find that little weasel and pound him until he-"

The tall blond guy threw his hand up to silence the hoodie kid.

"Shh," he commanded.

Everyone listened. The only obvious sound was the swirling prewinter wind rushing through the trees.

"What?" Hoodie snarled, impatiently. "A storm's coming. So what?"

The blond guy smiled. "Storm's already here. He's driving straight into it."

That's when they all heard it. The rumbling. What at first could only be sensed by the blond ring-leader was now obvious to everybody.

"That's him," the girl with the purple streak said with a mischievous grin. "It's on."

Another car turned off the road and into the parking lot where the group stood waiting. The throaty growl of its engine drowned out the steady sound of the chilly wind.

"Oh yeah," the blond guy said with satisfaction. "It's definitely on."

_____

"Theo!" I exclaimed.

He had answered his cell phone. Finally. I ran out of the kitchen and went straight up the stairs for his bedroom. I didn't want Harry to hear what I had to say.

Lu was right behind me.

"Where have you been?" Theo asked anxiously. "I've been calling you all morning."

"I know, I'm sorry," I said. "My battery died. Lu's here too."

"She wasn't answering either," Theo said. "But it's okay. It's over. You'll never believe where I am. Joe drove us out to—"

"It's not you, Theo," I said.

"Uh . . . what?" Theo asked, off-balance. "What do you mean?"

"It's your father," I said bluntly. "Your mother, too, for all I know. They're the ones in trouble."

I got nothing from the other end of the phone but silence. I guess I should have been a little gentler about the way I broke the news to him, but there were more important things going on. I waited for him to process the information, though I was afraid we were running out of time.

"Theo?" I finally said to make sure we hadn't been cut off.

"What're you talking about?" Theo said with confusion. "My birthday present was a helicopter ride. Joe and I are at the Stony Brook airport. It's a *red* helicopter! I'm looking at it right now. That's the red thing that crashes. It's gotta be. It has nothing to do with my father."

"A helicopter!" Lu exclaimed, leaning over my shoulder. "You're not going up in that thing, are you?"

"Of course not!" Theo said. "I refused, but it didn't matter. The pilot had already canceled the flight because of all the wind."

I felt Lu tense up next to me. I knew exactly what she was thinking.

"The pilot canceled the flight?" I asked. "You didn't ask him to do it?"

"I didn't have to," Theo replied. "It's way too dangerous to fly."

"Then it's definitely not about that helicopter, T," I said. "It can't be. If the pilot canceled the trip, it means you had nothing to do with changing things. You were never meant to go up. That wasn't your future. Nothing's changed. I'm telling you—I saw your dad on Face-Time two minutes ago. He was wearing a bright blue shirt. I thought the image in the crystal ball was you, but it was him. Whatever's going to happen, it's gonna be to him."

"But how? Why?" Theo exclaimed. "It wasn't his fortune."

Lu yanked the phone out of my hand.

"What did the fortune say, Theo? *Life as you know it will end on your fourteenth birthday.* If something happens to your father, to your parents, life as you know it will definitely change."

"Yeah, and what was the last word?" I asked, leaning into Lu to get to the phone.

"*Humility,*" Theo said.

"Exactly!" I exclaimed. "Humility. It's not about you, T. We've been so focused on you, we never thought of who else might be affected by that fortune."

Theo didn't say anything right away. I knew he was tugging on his ear, thinking. Calculating.

"Where are they?" he finally asked.

"They went to a diner for breakfast after church," Lu replied.

"The Silver Star," Theo said, suddenly all business. He had clicked into Theo-logical mode. "It's about a half mile from Saint Paul's. We always walk there after Mass. They'll be headed back to the church to pick up the car."

"So we can get to them at the church?" I asked.

"Yeah," Theo said. "But what are we gonna tell them?"

"Who cares?" I yelled. "Let's make sure they're safe first."

"We're at your house, Theo," Lu said. "Harry's here too. We'll get him to drive us to the church."

"I'll go straight there with Joe," Theo said. "We're still way out at the airport. You'll get there before I will."

"We're leaving right now," I said.

"Marcus? We can't let this fortune come true," Theo said, his voice cracking with emotion.

"We won't," I said with false bravado. "Go!"

I took the phone and ended the call.

"What're we gonna say to Harry?" Lu asked.

"We'll tell him we need a ride to church."

THE THROATY GROWL OF the powerful car engine was a rude disruption to the quiet suburban morning. The Corvette Stingray pulled into the school parking lot and rolled all the way to the far end, where the group of teens stood waiting. It stopped with its nose only a few inches from the grille of the black Mustang, intruding on its space. Menacing.

The kids stood around, most with their arms folded, trying to look badass. The driver killed the engine, and the neighborhood went eerily silent.

The driver's door of the Corvette opened, and a kid not much older than sixteen popped out. He had a thick shock of neon-orange-dyed hair that stood up on his head like he'd been hit with a solid jolt of electricity. Though it was chilly, he only wore an age-faded black AC/DC T-shirt and jeans. He shot up out of the car with so much energy it was like he'd just pounded down a gallon of coffee followed by a liter of Mountain Dew. His jaw was constantly working on a wad of gum.

"Yeah yeah!" he shouted exuberantly. "Didn't think you clowns would show!"

"You're calling us clowns, with that hair?" the kid with the hoodie said, scoffing.

The group of teens stared back at the new arrival

intently, as if trying to intimidate him. Or to prove his crazy attitude wasn't threatening them.

"You're late," the blond kid said. "Street's gonna get real busy real soon."

"Won't matter," the wild-eyed kid said. "This won't take long. Where's your driver?"

The girl with the purple streak in her dark hair stepped forward.

"Does your daddy know you took his car?" she asked.

The orange-haired, wild-eyed kid furiously worked his gum, glanced down at his 'Vette, and laughed.

"Ooh, disrespect!" he exclaimed. "From a girl with a grandma ride."

A few of the kids chuckled but quickly stifled themselves.

"It's not about the ride–it's about guts," the girl said.

The wild guy gave her a big Joker-like grin. "Yeah yeah. Let's find out who's got 'em."

The two stared each other down. The girl was laser-focused; the guy looked ready to burst out laughing.

"Start right here," the blond kid said. "Side by side. Take it to the far end of the parking lot. Straight-ahead sprint. Turn right onto the road. That's your track. From there keep making left turns until you do a full circle. Finish line is the entrance to the parking lot."

"I know the course," the wild-eyed guy said.

"So do I," the girl added.

"Then let's fly!" the orange-haired kid exclaimed with a giddy laugh.

The kids all whooped and cheered, forgetting how annoyed they were at having had to get up so early on a cold Sunday morning.

The Mustang was already in position. It was backed against a fence with its nose pointed toward the hundred-yard stretch of empty parking lot. The orange-haired kid ducked back into his Corvette and gunned the engine to impress (or intimidate) the others. He backed up, swung the car around, and eased into position next to the Mustang.

The girl fired up her engine. Its deep roar matched that of the 'Vette. These were two very powerful, very fast muscle cars. They couldn't idle there much longer or the sound would surely wake the neighbors. This was a quiet neighborhood . . .

. . . that wouldn't be quiet much longer.

The cars sat side by side, rumbling, aching to launch and run.

Two beautiful machines.

A jet-black Mustang.

And a fire-engine-red Corvette.

"Can you go a little faster?" I asked Harry. Pleaded, actually.

"What's the hurry?" he asked.

"It's cold," Lu said. "Maybe we'll see them walking back from the diner. We can give them a ride."

I was sitting in the passenger seat, and Lu was in the back. Harry turned around and gave her a confused look.

"They make that walk in a foot of snow," he said. "A little cold won't kill 'em."

"Let's hope not," I said. "Hurry, please."

All I wanted to do was get to the McLeans and surround them in some kind of protective cocoon. Between me and Lu and Theo and Theo's two brothers, we'd make sure that nothing happened to them. I kept telling myself we had control. The future wasn't set. That's not how life worked. But we had the advantage of knowing what might happen. Sort of.

It was a gift from the Oracle Baz. We couldn't waste it.

MR. AND MRS. McLEAN finished their breakfast, paid the bill, bundled up, and left the Silver Star diner for

263

the half-mile walk back to Saint Paul's Church. It was a pleasant walk along suburban sidewalks that they'd made a hundred times before . . . a tradition they had started long before their boys were born.

The wind kicked up, sending a blast of cold air their way. The two had to lean against each other for fear of getting knocked sideways.

"Whoa!" Mr. McLean exclaimed. "Where did that come from?"

He put his arm around his wife to ward off the piercing cold blast.

"I don't like this," Mrs. McLean said. "It's dangerous to be flying around in a helicopter with this wind."

"I hear you," Mr. McLean said. "Russell knows what he's doing. If it's too risky, he won't go up."

"Would you please call?" Mrs. McLean asked. "I want to know they're safe."

"We'll call from the car. I don't want to be out in this wind either."

They trudged on, bundled against the cold, holding tight to one another to stay warm as they made their way back to the church.

IN THE SCHOOL PARKING lot a quarter mile from Saint Paul's Church, the two cars sat next to one another, their engines revving.

The orange-haired kid behind the wheel of the red Corvette waved playfully to the girl in the black Mustang. "Yeah yeah!" he exclaimed with a wild laugh.

The girl ignored him. One hand gripped the wheel, the other the gearshift. She was focused and ready to go.

Most of the other kids had run to the entrance of the parking lot. Their job was to stop any car that might be coming their way as the racers turned onto the street. It was the only safety precaution planned. Once the racers were on the course, they were on their own.

The blond kid stood five yards in front of the two cars. He looked to the 'Vette and put his hand to his ear.

The Corvette's driver responded by revving his engine.

The blond kid gave him a thumbs-up, then looked to his friend behind the wheel of the Mustang. He made the same motion.

The girl pumped her gas. Her engine roared.

She too got a thumbs-up. The blond kid stood with his arms at his sides. Slowly, he raised them both until his hands were directly overhead.

The drivers gunned their engines again.

They were ready.

It was on.

The blond kid hesitated for a long two seconds and . . .

"Go!" he shouted, and dropped both arms.

The drivers jammed their gas pedals to the floor and released their clutches. With a squeal of rubber on blacktop, the cars lurched forward, shooting by the blond kid who stood stock-still for fear of getting run over. He was quickly enveloped in a cloud of pungent smoke from burned rubber. Once the cars sped by him, he spun to watch as the two vehicles screamed away, side by side, each gunning to be the first out of the parking lot.

The Mustang was on the right, the same direction they would have to turn. If they hit the exit at the same time, one of them would have to back off and let the other go first, or it would be a violent end to a very short race.

The other kids stood on the street, cheering the drivers on.

The cars accelerated toward the exit, neck and neck.

Somebody had to blink.

It wasn't the kid in the Corvette. With a maniacal laugh, he spun the steering wheel and made the turn without slowing or downshifting.

The girl in the Mustang had no choice but to hit the brakes. She slowed, and the Corvette shot across her front grille, headed out onto the road.

The tone was set and the race was on.

Most everyone who lived nearby in the quiet neighborhood had no idea of what was happening on their streets. Some might have heard distant squeals or engine sounds, but none paid attention. Most were still in bed asleep. It was the exact reason why these kids had chosen this course. They'd scouted it. They knew it was not only a perfect mile-long course that was easy to follow, but the chances of anybody getting in their way were slim to none because of the hour and the quiet time between early-morning Masses.

They had the course to themselves.

Except for the couple who were walking toward the racecourse, huddled together, bundled against the cold, with no idea of what was headed their way.

CHAPTER

21

THE MUSTANG HAD MORE horsepower than the Corvette, but the Corvette was more nimble. The black car caught up with the red in seconds. The girl would have blown right by the orange-haired guy if they hadn't reached the first left turn of the course.

The red Corvette made the sharp turn without slowing, its wide wheels gripping the blacktop without a slip.

The girl had to downshift to slow quickly or she wouldn't have made the turn. Her wheels squealed on the pavement as she sideslipped toward the curb. But she kept control, finished the turn, and charged on.

The fast turn gave the Corvette precious seconds to jump farther ahead on the second leg of the "track" as it screamed along the empty suburban street. Once the Mustang finished the turn, the girl instantly jammed down the gas pedal. The powerful engine roared as the black car picked up speed, charging to catch up with the smaller sports car.

We didn't say much for the rest of the drive to the church. It wasn't like we were going to explain to Harry all that was really happening. But my mind was working fast, thinking ahead to how we might keep the McLeans safe for the rest of the day. One thing I knew for sure: I'd get Mr. McLean to change his shirt.

"What's that sound?" Lu asked.

She rolled down the window, and we all listened to hear what sounded like a loud engine running somewhere in the neighborhood.

"Leaf blower?" I said. "You're not supposed to use those on Sunday."

"And the wind is blowing everything around anyway," Lu said.

"Sounds like a car engine," Harry said. "Maybe two. They're revving pretty high."

The sound grew louder. We were only a block or two

from Saint Paul's Church. My mind quickly went ahead to try and guess what might be making this sound. Whatever it was, I didn't think it would be good.

And I was right.

"Whoa!" Harry exclaimed.

He slammed on the brakes and the car bucked to a stop, forcing us all forward against our seat belts. A second later two cars blew by in front of us, left to right, through the intersection we had been approaching. They were really hauling, too, way over the speed limit.

Two cars. One black and one red.

Lu grabbed my shoulder.

"You saw that, right?" she asked.

"Hard to miss," Harry said, sounding shaken. "Idiots! What are they doing?"

"Racing," I said.

"They're gonna kill somebody," Harry said.

I glanced back to Lu.

The look on her face was one of realization . . . and panic.

"Should we try to stop them?" Lu asked.

"Why?" Harry exclaimed. "You want to get killed too?"

"No, let's get to the church," I said. "Gotta make sure your parents are okay."

Harry shot me a worried look. He was with the program. He didn't know anything about fortunes or destiny or crystal balls, but he understood that if his parents were walking around in an area where two lunatics were drag racing, there could be a problem. He hit the gas and we launched forward.

———————

THE RACERS CHARGED ON down the empty street.

The black Mustang caught up to the Corvette quickly, but once again the fast-handling Corvette was able to take the second left turn without dropping much speed.

The girl was right behind. She hit the turn faster than the last one to try and keep up with the red car, but she ended up in a dangerous side-slip. With smoke billowing from its squealing wheels, the Mustang drifted toward the side of the street. The girl was seconds from hitting the curb when her wheels finally bit and got traction. It was a daring and dangerous maneuver to have taken the turn going that fast, but it paid off. It kept her from losing any more ground to the Corvette. She came out of the turn only a few car lengths back.

The little red car was now in her sights. With a deafening roar that was sure to wake the sleeping neighbors, the Mustang leapt ahead and passed the little car before they were halfway to the next turn. For the first time the Mustang was in the lead, with two more turns to go.

———————————

Harry took off through the intersection and made a left turn. It was the exact opposite direction from where the racing cars were headed and the quickest way for us to get to the church. So many thoughts and fears were running around in my head. The cars had come from the direction of the church. If the McLeans had been there, could they have been hit? Were the cars racing to get away from the scene of an accident? Was that how Theo's life was going to change? Or were the cars going to circle around and arrive back at the church at the same time as the McLeans?

The images from the crystal ball kept playing in my head. Mostly I remembered the red sheet metal hitting something hard and violently buckling. It was the same red as the Corvette. There was no doubt in my mind that whatever Baz's fortune had predicted, it would be about the car that was now recklessly tearing through the neighborhood. Whatever was supposed to happen hadn't happened yet.

Harry sped along and made a right turn onto the street that led to the church.

"Slow down," Lu warned Harry. "We're not the ones racing."

But Harry was on a mission.

"If anything happened to my parents because of those guys—"

"Look out!" I shouted.

As soon as we rounded the corner, too fast, we were faced with a group of older kids hanging out in the street. They looked totally clueless, as if they had no idea they were in the middle of the road.

We were moving so fast I thought for sure we'd mow a couple of them down, but Harry spun the wheel hard and hit the brakes. The car fishtailed, swerved, and bumped up and over the curb onto a sidewalk, where we came to rest.

"What the hell!" Harry screamed angrily. "You guys okay?"

"Yeah," I said.

"I'm good," Lu added.

Some of the kids ran away, weenies. But one kid came running over to us. He was tall, with short blond hair. He was the only one with any guts.

"Are you all right?" he asked excitedly.

Harry threw the car door open, jumped out, and stood up to the guy.

"What're you all doing in the middle of the road?" Harry screamed at him.

"It's a race," the blond guy said nervously. "Usually nobody's around. Sorry, man."

"Yeah, well *usually* ain't *always,* fool," Harry said angrily.

He went to the front of his car and saw that the left front tire was flat.

"Oh man, I am gonna catch it for this," he whined.

"You know those guys racing?" I asked the blond guy.

"Yeah. It's been a feud going on for a long time. We wanted to settle it today and finally put—"

"I don't care," I said sharply. "Which way are they going?"

"They're gonna circle around the block," he said. "Finish line is right here."

"They're gonna go right past the church," Lu said with dread.

I looked at Harry's car. Flat tire. Done. There was only one way to get to the church.

Run.

———————

"I'M FREEZING," MRS. MCLEAN said.

Mr. McLean immediately took off his overcoat and draped it over his wife's shoulders as they walked along the sidewalk.

"Now you're going to be chilled," she said, but didn't refuse the coat.

"I'll be fine," Mr. McLean said, though his thin blue shirt did nothing to protect him from the chilly wind. "We're almost there."

"Listen," Mrs. McLean said with curiosity. "What is that sound?"

They both focused and heard the roar of engines revving higher than normal. They seemed to be far off, but coming closer. Fast.

"Sounds like somebody's tearing up the street," Mr. McLean said. "I've heard stories about crazy kids drag racing around here because it's so quiet."

"Doesn't sound very quiet to me," Mrs. McLean said.

They were footsteps away from stepping onto the street that ran in front of the church ... the final straightaway of the racecourse.

THE CORVETTE WAS LOSING. The back straightaway before the third turn was the longest of the race, and it gave the Mustang a chance to show what it could do—and it was a lot. It opened up a big lead on the red Corvette, but there were still two more turns to go.

The orange-haired kid eased the Corvette into the left lane. The oncoming lane. He was setting

275

up to take the next turn even sharper than the last and turn inside the Mustang. If he pulled it off, the Mustang would have to slow down and make a wide turn. It was the only hope the Corvette had of taking back the lead.

"Yeah yeah, here I come!" the orange-haired kid screamed at nobody as he sped along the wrong side of the street.

The girl seemed to know exactly what he was trying to do. If she was going to have any hope of outmaneuvering the little sports car, she would have to take this next turn even faster than the last two. It was a big risk. She'd barely made the last turn without skidding off the road. But it was her only hope of winning.

They approached the turn doing nearly sixty miles an hour. Not that fast for a real racetrack, but on a flat suburban road, it was beyond reckless. The Mustang flew into the turn, cutting in front of the Corvette.

"No no no!" the orange-haired kid screamed in surprise.

The girl had boldly cut off any chance the Corvette had of taking the turn inside of her, for it would have broadsided the bigger car.

For the first time in the race, the orange-haired kid had to downshift. He decelerated fast, then popped the clutch to try and throw his car back into gear. But the high-performance car wasn't used to being treated so rudely, and the engine stalled.

Just like that, the Corvette was dead.

Or was it? The Mustang skid and slid, much the way it had on the previous turn. But this time the driver had pushed it too far. The car careened across the road, going more sideways than straight ahead. The girl tried to regain control, but the tires didn't cooperate and she kept drifting.

Behind her, the Corvette's engine roared back to life.

"Yeah yeah!" Orange Hair yelled with a laugh. "Here I come!"

He was seconds away from being back in the race.

MR. AND MRS. McLEAN reached the street that passed in front of the church and stepped off the curb to cross as . . .

The black Mustang slid into the turn, fifty yards to their left.

"My God!" Mrs. McLean said with a gasp.

"Fools," Mr. McLean added.

They watched the scene unfold, mesmerized, as they continued to slowly walk across the street.

Too slowly.

THE MUSTANG WAS DOOMED. The car slid sideways with no hope of regaining control. It hit the curb at a forty-five-degree angle, bounced up onto the sidewalk, and slammed straight into a fire hydrant. Instantly, multiple jets of water shot from the damaged device. A high-pressure geyser launched into the sky, fountain-like, while a steady stream of water spewed into the street ahead of the accident.

The McLeans stopped and watched, stunned, in the dead center of the road.

"This can't be happening," Mrs. McLean whispered in shock.

Lu and I sprinted along the sidewalk until we got to the empty parking lot of Saint Paul's Church.

"That's their car!" Lu exclaimed.

There was a single car in the vast parking lot. A maroon Volvo wagon. The McLeans'.

"So where are they?" I asked.

Boom!

There was a screech, followed by what sounded like

a nasty collision . . . the kind I saw in the crystal ball. The violent shriek made us both jump with surprise.

The church was on the corner. Whatever had crashed, it was on the next street, around the corner, beyond the church, out of our sight. We didn't need to see it to know that something horrible had happened.

My heart sank.

"We're too late," Lu said softly.

I took off running through the church property, going behind the building to cut the corner and get to the street beyond. Lu kept pace. I dreaded what we would find.

We ran from behind the church and onto the sidewalk of the next street to witness the mayhem. Far to our right, maybe fifty yards away, Mr. and Mrs. McLean stood in the middle of the street, staring at the destruction. Mr. McLean was wearing a bright blue shirt, just like the one I saw in the crystal ball.

Check.

The sight made my stomach twist.

"They're okay!" Lu exclaimed.

I wasn't ready to celebrate. Another fifty yards beyond them was the accident scene. A black Mustang was up on the curb next to a fire hydrant that was spewing water everywhere. Water. Just like I saw in the crystal ball.

Check.

It was obvious that the car had skidded off the road and hit the hydrant.

"It's over, right?" Lu said hopefully. "The McLeans are okay. They weren't in the accident."

As if in answer, another car came screaming around the corner behind the crashed Mustang. It was the red Corvette.

"Unless there's gonna be another accident," I said, and took off running for the McLeans.

"Get out of the road!" I shouted.

They must have had a deer-in-the-headlights thing going on, because they didn't budge. They were square in the middle of the road with a high-powered car headed right for them. A red car.

Check. Check. Check.

"Move!" Lu screamed.

It seemed as though Lu's shout woke them up. They finally snapped out of it and moved. The two hugged each other while hurrying to the right side of the road, and safety.

We had intervened. We had changed the future.

"We did it," Lu exclaimed. "They're gonna make it!"

But the Mustang wasn't done. It suddenly sprang to life and bounced back onto the road . . . directly in the path of the oncoming Corvette. The Mustang wasn't moving anywhere near as fast as the red car, so the Corvette was on it in a second.

We hadn't changed a thing. The accident I'd seen in the crystal ball hadn't happened yet.

But it was about to.

I cringed, waiting for a collision.

There was a squeal of brakes. The Mustang accelerated and the Corvette had to brake or it would have slammed into it from behind. At the exact moment the driver of the Corvette hit the brakes, the red car reached the water that had spread across the road. It was like trying to stop on a sheet of ice. The Corvette kept coming, skidding sideways at full speed, wheels spinning, heading straight for the McLeans, who hadn't yet made it to the safety of the sidewalk.

"Oh my God, no!" Lu exclaimed.

It seemed like it was all happening in slow motion. The confusing images I had seen in the crystal ball were being knit together into one horrible whole. All the missing pieces of the puzzle, pieces that Baz hadn't needed to see in order to understand what would happen, had now shown themselves.

The crushing truth became clear. As much as we tried to beat it, destiny was too powerful. It couldn't be changed. We were just spectators going along for the ride, pretending the things we did mattered. But they didn't, because we were just actors walking through our own predetermined dramas.

It was a dark, disturbing realization that was about to be driven home by the deaths of two innocent people.

Lu buried her head in my shoulder. She didn't want to see.

Too bad, because she missed seeing the ultimate puzzle piece slipping into place. It was a piece that wasn't expected or foreseen. This last piece proved that destiny was not an inescapable life sentence after all.

We really did have control.

Theo came sprinting toward his parents from the back end of the church property, running faster than I'd ever seen him move in his life. His parents were focused on the Mustang as it sped off, thinking they'd dodged a bullet. They had no idea the Corvette was careening toward them from behind.

But Theo knew.

He ran in like a charging linebacker and hit his parents without breaking stride. He locked up and drove forward, knocking them back into the road. The three fell to the wet pavement as the Corvette skidded by, its wheels spinning uselessly. It slammed into the curb, which finally stopped the car's forward motion. There was no crumpling of red metal. There was no crash. No-body's life was changed.

Theo had made sure of that.

The guy driving the car looked like a kid . . . with orange hair that was all spiked up like it was on fire.

Final check. Or maybe I should say checkmate.

I thought he'd jump out of the car to make sure everybody was okay, but all he did was slam his fists into the steering wheel in frustration. He then hit the gas and took off. Tool.

The Mustang driver wasn't any better. She had no clue about how close she'd come to disaster and I'm guessing she didn't care. When the Mustang flew by us, I took note because I knew the police would ask about it. I wanted to remember the girl behind the wheel with long dark hair that had a purple streak in it. The Mustang was followed soon after by the red car. The Corvette. There was no mistaking that one and the orange hair of the driver. I planned on doing everything I could to help the police find those two jackwagons.

The two cars continued past the church and made the left turn that would bring them to their finish line. Part of me was actually happy about it. If things had played out the way Baz had predicted, they never would have finished the race, and two people would be dead. Maybe more.

But nobody died. Life as we all knew it would go on. Thanks to Theo.

Lu and I ran to the three people who were lying in the street.

Joe McLean ran up. Harry joined us too. The four of us stood over Theo and his parents. They all had their arms wrapped around each other.

There was a tense moment when nobody knew what to say.

Finally, Theo turned his head and looked up at us. "So?" he said with a big smile. "Can I get a 'happy birthday'?"

CHAPTER

22

"This one's yours, T," I said to Theo. "You earned it."

Theo couldn't help but smile. He'd been waiting for me to say that.

"I'd call it *Oracle of Doom*," he said with conviction.

"Whoa," Lu said, chuckling. "Drama."

"Well, yeah," Theo said with a shrug.

Everett looked to me, I nodded, and he slid the black book across the circulation desk of the Library toward me.

"*Oracle of Doom* it is," he said, and handed me the ancient black pen I had used to sign out the book to begin our adventure.

I knew the drill. With Theo and Lu watching, I opened the front cover of the book to reveal the card

I had signed that allowed me, an agent of the Library, to check out the book and enter the story. With one bold swipe of the pen, I crossed out my name. With that, the book now called *Oracle of Doom* was complete, and Everett could move it from the shelf with all the unfinished books, to the finished section.

"How are you going to categorize it?" Theo asked.

Everett took the book and held it to his chest as if it was precious, and in some ways it was, because it represented the completion of multiple disruptions.

The mystery of Baz's death had been solved, allowing his spirit to be released from Playland. The truth had been revealed that Eugene Derby had nothing to do with the fire and Baz's death, which also allowed his spirit to be freed. Lu's cousin had been found, though she was never in any danger. Most important, the McLeans were safe, and Theo's life as he knew it would go on.

It was only one book, but we finished a whole lot of stories. Not too bad.

"I believe this will go under the heading *Fortune*," Everett said.

"Fortune? How do you figure that?" Lu asked. "Because Baz was a fortune-teller?"

Everett rolled off his stool and lumbered around the desk, headed for one of the aisles that held the completed books.

"In part," he said. "But fortune can mean a lot of things. It's about destiny and fate. Even luck. Many of the stories here in the Library are about folks whose fortunes have taken a turn for the worse. Their stories will never be finished until they come to realize that fortune is truly in their own hands."

"Or somebody from the Library helps them figure it out," Theo said.

"Aye," Everett said. "Everybody needs a little help sometime."

He slipped the book between two others on the shelf and came back to the desk.

"You all did a fine thing here," Everett added. "For the spirits in the story and for yourselves."

"Too bad that Daring Donna lady never got caught for what she did," Lu said. "In real life, I mean."

"Aye, but now the truth is known," Everett said. "Hers is a spirit that may no longer be resting in peace."

"What about those idiots who were drag racing?" Theo asked.

"The police are all over it," I said. "Lu and I told them everything we saw, and there's video from security cameras at the church and the middle school. They're not gonna be driving anywhere for a while."

"Then I guess we're done here," Lu said, and moved to get up.

"Wait," Theo said. "I don't know if it's too late to make this part of the book, but I want you guys to know how much I appreciate what you did for me."

"You're the one who saved your parents," I said.

"But you wouldn't let me give up," he said. "I felt really helpless, like there was nothing I could do to save myself. But you two wouldn't listen."

"We *never* listen to anything you say," Lu said with a straight face.

Theo gave her a hurt look, but she smiled and squeezed his arm.

"I'm kidding," she said. "I just couldn't believe our lives are planned out like some movie script, no matter what a crystal ball says. Nobody's future is written."

"And like I said, we make our own fortunes," Everett added.

"You think that machine at Playland is still going to spit out predictions even though Baz's spirit is gone?" Theo asked.

"We could always go back next summer and find out," I said.

We all looked at one another, then burst out laughing.

"Yeah, right," I exclaimed. "Like *that's* gonna happen."

"No way," Theo added.

"I'll pass," Lu said.

There was nothing left to do except get back to real life.

"What're you thinking, Marcus?" Everett asked. "Will I be seeing you again soon?"

Theo and Lu both looked my way. They wanted to know too.

"I need a break," I said. "We all do. It's been pretty intense. I still want to get into what really happened to my birth parents, but I also think we should go back to being normal for a while."

"Can't argue with that," Theo said.

"Sounds good to me," Lu added.

"I'll keep hunting for any stories that might tell us something about your folks," Everett offered.

"Thanks, Everett," I said.

"Then we'll say good-bye," I said. "For now."

The three of us got up and headed for the door that would lead into my bedroom. Part of me was relieved. I really did need a break. The idea of sitting in a boring classroom, listening to a lecture on something I didn't care about, was actually sounding pretty good right about then.

On the other hand, I also had a wistful feeling. We

were leaving a library filled with unfinished adventures. What else was waiting for us on those shelves? Where would we go next? Whose story would we try to finish? I had gotten a taste of what it was like to jump into these stories, and to be perfectly honest, I liked it. Leaving it behind made me feel as though I might be missing out.

"Lots of books in this Library," Everett said. "They'll all be here waiting when you get back."

It was like he had read my mind.

"See you soon," I said, and led my friends through the door and back to normal life.

We stepped into my bedroom and I closed the door behind us. Just to be sure, I re-opened the door and took a quick peek inside to see . . . my closet. Without the Paradox key, it was just an ordinary closet door.

"What day is it again?" Lu asked, half-serious. "I've lost track."

"Monday morning," Theo said. "We've got school."

"Oh," Lu said, sounding disappointed. "That. How . . . dull."

It did sound dull. Perfectly, wonderfully dull.

We grabbed our packs from my bed and headed downstairs. We were alone in the house, since my parents had already left for work. It was shaping up to be a bland, normal day.

I opened the front door and stood back for my friends to go through first, but neither moved.

"What's that?" Lu asked.

Sitting outside the door was a cardboard box about the size of a big gym bag. I leaned outside to get a closer look and saw that there was something written in bold letters on top:

FOR: MR. MARCUS O'MARA

"That's you," Theo said.

"Yeah, no kidding," I said, and reached down to pick it up. The box wasn't all that heavy. "There's no return address. No shipping address either. Somebody must have dropped it off."

"It's not your birthday," Lu said. "Is it?"

I put the box down on the floor inside the house while Theo closed the door. The three of us stood around the mystery box, staring at it in wonder.

"Well, it's not going to open itself up," Lu said.

I took my house key out of my pocket and used it like a knife to cut the paper sealing tape. When I lifted the flaps, a sharp odor drifted out. It wasn't bad, but it was definitely strong.

"Ooh, weird," Theo said. "It smells like the beach."

"Yeah," Lu added. "Like seaweed."

The contents were covered by a sheet of brown paper, on top of which was a beige envelope with *Marcus* written in fancy, old-fashioned lettering.

"Sure looks like a birthday present to me," Lu said.

"Yeah," Theo said, sniffing. "Maybe somebody sent you some fresh lobsters."

I opened the envelope and slipped out a heavy paper card that had the same fancy handwriting on it. It said:

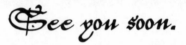

"That's it?" Lu asked. " 'See you soon'? Not who it's from?"

Lu and Theo each took the card to examine it, but there was nothing more to see except the simple message.

" 'See you soon,' " I read again, as if it might make more sense the second time.

"So what's in there?" Lu asked.

I knelt down and reached into the box to pull away the brown paper that was covering the contents. I can honestly say that I had no idea what I would find, not even with the definite ocean smell that drifted out. I didn't think for a second that it would be something that was going to turn my world inside out. Again. The thought never entered my mind.

But it should have.

I pulled the brown paper away.

Theo gasped.

Lu let out a squeal of surprise.

I could only stare, trying to get my brain to unlock and come up with some kind of logical explanation for what I was seeing.

Theo fell to his knees and said, "It's impossible."

"No . . . no way," Lu said, backing off as if being repelled by an invisible force field.

I didn't pull it out of the box. I didn't have to. There was no mistaking what it was. The scratches on its surface were proof. The smell too. I knew exactly what it was. What I didn't know was how it got there.

We were staring at a World War II–era ammunition box. Green. Standard issue. The marks on its surface were from the chains we had fastened around it and locked tight before dumping it into the deep waters of the Long Island Sound. It was never supposed to be found, its contents never seen again.

Or so we had hoped.

But the box was here.

It was open.

And it was empty.

The Boggin had escaped.